THE DEAL

Mickey spoke into the phone. "Yeah, it's good. Let 'em have the weapons." He hung up and held out his hand to Rostov. "Pleasure doing business with you, man."

Rostov smiled. "The pleasure is all mine." His right hand lashed out, his open palm striking Tina on the back of her head, driving the gold straw up her nose.

Not giving Mickey a chance to react, Rostov grabbed him by the throat and yanked the .45 from Mickey's belt and fired five shots through the door. Slowly the door swung open to reveal Mickey's bodyguards slumped on the ground. He jammed the .45 back into Mickey's belt and fired three times into his crotch. Then he grabbed Tina by her hair and flung her forward through the dirty window. Glass exploded outward as she sailed through, screaming as she plummeted to the sidewalk.

Rostov calmly surveyed his work and nodded with satisfaction.

JASON FROST

PINNACLE BOOKS   NEW YORK

This novel is a work of fiction. Names, characters, places, and incidents are either the product of the author's imagination or are used fictitiously. Any resemblance to actual events or places or persons, living or dead, is entirely coincidental.

INVASION U.S.A.

Copyright © 1985 by Cannon Films

An original Pinnacle Books edition, published for the first time anywhere.

First printing/October 1985

ISBN: 0-523-42669-0
Can. ISBN: 0-523-43608-4

Printed in the United States of America

PINNACLE BOOKS, INC.
1430 Broadway
New York, New York 10018

9 8 7 6 5 4 3 2 1

INVASION
U.S.A.

1

There was blood on her hands.

"Is it safe?" Domingo asked her.

"Safe?" Angela said. She returned her bleeding hand to the thick wooden tiller, gripping it tightly. Blood squeezed out of the open calluses and soaked into the old weather-beaten wood. The pain was like sharp nails being hammered into her palms, but she showed no sign of it to the others. It was best that Domingo didn't see the blood or calluses. He would insist on taking the tiller himself, and he was not as good a sailor as she.

"Angela," he repeated. "Is it safe?"

"Yes, the mast is safe. If the weather remains kind, it will not break."

"That, at least, is a blessing."

"Blessing!" Miguel sneered, his thin, bony body hunched against the taffrail. "It would be a blessing if we had never left Cuba. The food is gone, the water will be gone by noon. We are twenty-eight people squeezed into a broken-down boat that could barely hold twenty-eight *fish*. Pirates roam these waters. And if the Americans catch us, they will send us back to Cuba.''

Juan, a young boy of thirteen, looked up with fear. ''Is that true, Angela? If the Americans catch us, they will send us back?''

Angela smiled at her little brother. ''They will not catch us.''

Miguel started to say something, but a sharp look from Angela silenced him. She studied what was left of the stars, keeping the tiny sailboat aimed toward Florida. The sky was still dark, but the morning sun was already peeling back the edges of night along the eastern horizon.

Angela's hands had gripped the tiller so long last night that even when Domingo took his turn so she could sleep, she'd still felt the pressure of the round wood against her empty palms. After that, she'd given up trying to sleep at all.

Now she looked out over the other refugees: old couples, young couples, orphaned children. Some might not survive this coming day. Their eyes looked dull, their skin dry and flaking from the punishment of sun and salt air.

Angela had had several opportunities to make this trip before. Many from her village had gone, never to be heard from again. Sometimes she read in the newspapers about the sunken ships, the dead Cuban bodies, half-eaten, washed up on the clean white beaches of fancy Miami hotels. But the newspapers never printed stories about those who made it. Domingo had been telling her that ever since their marriage five years ago, always trying to convince her. He was the optimistic one. She was the sensible one.

Her father had told her she had the blood of Cortez in her veins. Cortez had been assistant to the governor of

2

Cuba in 1518 when he set out to conquer Montezuma and the Aztecs. He'd been thirty-three. Same age as she. Now Angela, too, was setting out, not because of Cortez, or even Domingo, but because of the baby, barely three months old, growing inside of her. The baby deserved a better life. She had not even told Domingo, knowing he would become fearful for her, for his child, and not want to risk the dangerous voyage. No, better to tell him later, when they were safe in Miami.

Miguel fidgeted with the tiny transistor radio. Everyone watched him, a dim glow of hope in their tired eyes. Static crackled. He adjusted the tuner with the delicacy of a safecracker. A fragmented voice would be heard, then fade tauntingly. Then, suddenly, one voice broke through.

"Rockin' talkin' Danny DePesto comin' at ya. The Ruler of Records, the Pope of Platters, the Goon with the Tune, the Maestro of Miami, givin' ya the solid-gold hits . . ."

A loud cheer drowned out the rest of the d.j.'s words as the refugees hugged and kissed each other. Laughter cut through the night, the chilly breeze. The happy sounds seemed strange to Angela, for she had not heard laughter since that first day when the greasy engine had sputtered and coughed and died.

"Solid-gold hits!" Domingo mimicked in broken English, then laughed.

"In America, everything is gold," young Juan put in. "The streets are paved with gold."

"They are not paved with gold," Miguel said.

"At least they are paved," Angela said.

Even Miguel smiled at that.

The radio crackled with Cyndi Lauper's "Girls Just Want to Have Fun." Old Carlo pulled his blanket tighter

3

around his ninety-four-year-old shoulders and began humming with the radio. His wife held his hand and hummed with him. Soon others joined in, humming with the words they couldn't understand. Some made up Spanish lyrics. Little Juan pulled out his bamboo flute and played along.

They all stared straight ahead as if at any minute they expected to see Florida's welcoming shores.

"America," Domingo sighed, as if that word said it all.

Everyone nodded agreement.

"A boat! A boat!" Juan yelled, pointing wildly.

Angela cupped a hand over her eyes and squinted into the rising sun. Indeed a boat was coming straight at them, its night lights still shining. She couldn't tell what kind of boat yet. Automatically she stiffened; one blistered hand went to her stomach to assure the baby.

"Angela?" Juan asked.

"Shhh." She had no answers for him.

Domingo put his arm around her shoulder. She felt better.

No one spoke. No one breathed.

They watched the distant boat speeding toward them, bullying water out of its way.

"The flag!" Juan cried. "It's American."

"Thank God," Angela said.

"Thank God?" Miguel spat. "The Americans will send us home."

"Maybe not," Angela said. "But even if they do, we will come back again. And again." She looked lovingly into Domingo's eyes. He smiled at her. "And again."

Miguel shrugged. "You are right, Angela. It could have been worse. It could have been Cuban. Then there would have been no return."

The other refugees sagged with resignation. The whole boat seemed to sink slightly in the ocean.

"Do not worry," Angela told them all cheerfully. "Cuba has thirty-seven hundred islands and cays. We will hide on one until we try again."

They stared sadly at her.

Except for Old Carlo. He threw off his blanket and began waving it at the coming ship, clearly a U.S. Coast Guard cutter.

"What are you doing, old man?" Miguel asked.

"Welcoming our guests. Today we welcome them. Tomorrow"—he shrugged—"perhaps the other way around."

Soon everyone was happily waving hands or clothing at the approaching ship.

Angela held the tiller steady as Domingo lowered the sail. The larger ship pulled along their tiny creaking boat, which she had bought from that bandit Castillo for far too much money. She looked up at the bulwark and saw the tall captain, flanked on either side by a stiff-backed crewman. The sun was directly behind them, so Angela couldn't make out the faces. But the uniforms said it all: crisp, clean, no wrinkles, they bespoke the promise of America. She touched her stomach again and smiled up at the captain. She couldn't see his eyes under his hat, but she saw him return the smile. She sighed. Finally, she could relax her vigilance.

The captain checked his watch, tugged his left sleeve down, and nodded. Two other crewmen with rifles on their backs threw lines into the tiny boat. Angela noticed that the men next to the captain were also armed with nasty-looking guns. She didn't blame them; she knew these waters were sailed by pirates and drug smugglers.

"Look at the guns, Angela," Juan said excitedly.

5

"Hurry, Juan," she urged, ushering him toward the bow where the refugees were preparing to disembark.

Old Carlo was first. He was the oldest; he was the kindest. The best amongst them.

The captain of the Coast Guard cutter leaned over the railing to offer a helping hand to the old fisherman. Angela felt a tear of happiness at the sight. The captain smiled, his clean pale hand closing around Old Carlo's dark leathery one.

Then everything went wrong.

The captain's other hand suddenly swung around from behind his back. In it was a huge pistol, big and black like a crow. Still smiling, he pressed the muzzle against Old Carlo's confused face and fired. Blood and brain and chips of bone splashed back over the others. Angela felt a sharp splinter of skull stick in her cheek like a bee sting. Warm blood, either hers or Old Carlo's, dripped like syrup down her face.

Now all four crewmen joined their captain, their weapons clattering in harsh harmony as they fired into the helpless crowd. Some of the refugees jumped overboard, but these were immediately shot. Others merely knocked against each other in panic. They too were shot.

Angela watched all in a confused haze, as if she were the bride at a wedding where she recognized no one, least of all the groom. She saw a bullet drill through Miguel's throat, the blood spraying out the back of his neck like bright fireworks. He flipped overboard like a giddy child. As he floated there face down, a fat fish swam up from the deep and began nibbling at the hole in his neck.

Next to her, four shots hammered into Domingo's T-shirt. His chest collapsed like a mud slide. He tried to say something to Angela as he fell, but then he too was dead.

Angela grabbed Juan and pushed him down atop other bodies. Just as she did, she felt a pain in her stomach and wondered if the baby could possibly be kicking already. Then she saw the blood. A large bullet had chewed through her belly. She fell down. Her first thought was a hope that the bullet had missed the baby. She had never been shot before and was surprised at how fiery hot the wound felt.

The shooting continued. Angela felt Juan squirming beneath her. But he was not shot. She stilled him with a sharp pinch.

The tall captain with the crisp uniform said something in a language that was not English or Spanish. Angela thought it sounded like Russian.

At the captain's words, all the guns but one stopped shooting. Through half-opened lids, she saw one crewman still firing into the already dead bodies. Someone called him Koyo. He was Oriental, his face a grim mask of hatred.

The captain, again tugging at his left sleeve, turned to one of the crewmen at his side. "Nikko!"

The man named Nikko rushed over to Koyo and grabbed the weapon out of his hands. The Oriental, face contorted with bloodlust, glared at Nikko. Nikko ignored him and carried the guns below deck.

Angela remained still, hardly breathing as she watched. Around her she could hear the moans of some of the wounded. Perhaps the ship would simply leave now. There was still a chance she could save Juan. Maybe the baby.

The tall captain marched over to one of the other crewmen, a short, muscular man whose face was soaked with sweat. He was fumbling with the cap of a medicine bottle. The captain yanked the bottle out of his hand, examined the contents, frowned, and threw it overboard. He spoke

7

rapidly in German to the man, addressing him as Kurt. When he was finished talking, the captain slapped Kurt. Kurt took one angry step toward the captain, but suddenly stopped, looked away.

Nikko appeared on deck again, dragging someone behind him. Angela immediately recognized Castillo, the man who'd sold her the boat. They spoke in Spanish.

"Mother of God," Castillo said, gazing out over the dead and mangled bodies. He quickly crossed himself.

"Where is it?" the tall captain asked.

But Castillo was too shocked to answer.

The captain grabbed Castillo by the throat. "Where?"

"The f-foredeck."

The captain checked his watch again and boarded the little sailboat. Kurt, the Oriental, and the last crewman followed him aboard. Nikko stayed on the cutter with Castillo.

Angela watched the four men march toward the bow, stepping on the bodies as if they were stones. Whenever they came to anyone stirring or moaning, they immediately shot him. The young one stopped suddenly and began pawing aside some of the bodies. Roughly he pulled pretty Juanetta out from under the other bodies and propped her against the mast. She was sixteen. Blood streamed down her left arm from a shoulder wound. She stared at him, frozen with fear, as he leeringly began unbuttoning her blouse. A small firm breast was revealed. She moved a hand to cover herself, but he batted it away, grabbing the breast with such force that she cried out in pain.

"Tomas!" the captain said coldly. When Tomas looked up, the captain lifted his gun and fired. His bullet punched through Juanetta's chest, inches from Tomas's hand. Her blood splattered across his knuckles.

Tomas laughed, wiped his hand on his pants, and caught up with the others.

Angela felt Juan shivering beneath her. She squeezed his hand, and he continued to play dead.

The captain pointed and the three crewmen began kicking aside bodies, throwing others overboard. Kurt and Tomas pried at the boards with crowbars. After a few minutes, the Oriental reached down into the hole and pulled up a plastic bag filled with white powder. Angela knew it was cocaine.

They loaded bag after bag into green duffel bags, tossing them up to Nikko. Angela had never seen so great a quantity of drugs before. She knew little of such matters, but suspected their worth was in the millions.

When the captain and his men had returned to their ship, Nikko kicked Castillo in the back, sending him plunging over the rail and into the sailboat. The boat rocked wildly, and again Angela felt the pain in her stomach. Still, she didn't move. Maybe they would leave now, leave them alone in the boat. She might yet get them to Miami. She closed her eyes, not wanting to take any chances.

"What are you doing?" Castillo screamed.

Angela heard a splashing sound, smelled the bitter scent of gasoline.

"You promised," Castillo begged. "You promised!"

The Coast Guard cutter pulled away, and she heard rough laughter. She opened her eyes again, saw Castillo's fat clumsy body running for the side of the boat as he tried to hurl himself over. But he tripped on the bodies and fell, crying.

Angela pushed herself up, hand clutched to her stomach. She tugged Juan after her. The smell of gasoline was thick and stinging. The fumes burned her eyes. She strug-

9

gled toward the side of the boat, dragging her brother behind.

Then she looked up and saw the tall captain in his crisp, clean uniform. He was smiling. Smiling as he raised the thick flare gun in both hands, aimed, and fired.

The blazing missile hurtled toward them like a fiery comet. Angela relaxed. She knew it was too late.

When the flare hit the gasoline-soaked bodies, the flames exploded in a twenty-foot wave of fire. As the blaze swept over Angela and Juan, she heard the final gasps of Miguel's transistor radio: "Rockin' talkin' Danny DePesto only nine shopping days before Christmas, playin' the latest, greatest from Kenny Loggins, hittin' the charts at number thirty-seven, bound to be another solid-gold hit . . ."

Then the heat melted the radio and Angela and the boat.

2

She began by unbuttoning her blouse. There was no other way. The cops were everywhere. "Christ, McGuire," she said to herself, looking out her car window. "Is there no limit with you?"

She noticed some fatty in a business suit who'd been watching all the squad cars and ambulances pull up to the docks. He was eating donuts from a white bag. Now that he saw what she was doing, he turned and gaped. Powdered sugar spotted his chin, hung on his lapels like dandruff.

She ignored him, continued thumbing buttons through buttonholes. She shrugged out of the blouse and quickly unhooked the front of her bra. She shrugged out of that too. The fatty was staring at her with his tongue half hanging out of his mouth. She gave him a bored look, pretended to stick her finger up her nose. He made a disgusted face and turned away.

Occupational hazard, she thought with a laugh. She pulled her blouse back on and rebuttoned it, but only to the tip of the sternum. There had to be plenty of cleavage if this was going to work.

She reached into the back seat, rooted among the five or six cameras there, selected a small 35mm Nikon, and stuffed it into her purse.

She climbed out of the car, adjusted her blouse for the most exposure, and began walking toward the young cop guarding the farthest perimeter from the action. She could see all the reporters bunched up near the dock entrance, bumping against each other as they pleaded and threatened with Lt. Green. He was shaking his head, probably telling them they'd have to wait for an official statement from the department. They'd groan and say something about the First Amendment. He'd loosen his tie and walk away.

"Grover," she called as she approached the young, bored-looking cop. "Here, Grover. Where are you, boy?" She whistled.

The cop looked at her, a smile splitting his already cynical face. She pretended not to notice him. She bent over and called "Grover" again. He stared down her blouse.

"You seen my dog?" she asked him.

"No, ma'am."

"Little dog. Part poodle, part something I haven't been able to identify yet. Garbage disposal, I think."

He grinned, reluctantly lifting his eyes from her breasts to her face. He was obviously just as pleased with what he saw there. "Haven't seen him. Sorry."

"There he is!" she said, pointing behind him.

The young cop turned and looked. "Where? I don't see anything."

"He ducked behind that ambulance. My goodness," she

said, as if noticing all the squad cars and ambulances for the first time. "What's going on here?"

His face got stony and professional. "Hope you find your dog, ma'am."

"Me, too, officer. He was a gift from my mother right before she died last month. Kind of a peace offering. Grover means a lot to me."

His face softened slightly. "Yeah, well . . ."

"Thing is, since we both saw him running over there, maybe I could just slip in and pick him up. I'd get right out of everybody's way. Poor Grover's probably sitting behind that car shivering with fear. He doesn't do so hot on his own. Not much of a watchdog either, but I live alone and, well, he's company."

He looked at her, weighing the risks and possible rewards, letting his eyes wash over her breasts while he made up his mind. Finally he stepped aside and lifted the rope. She ducked under it.

She headed straight for the dock. "Thanks." She waved back to him.

"You gotta find him and get right out again, okay?"

"You kidding? I don't want to hang around with all this fuss. Might screw up my pacemaker."

He gave her a funny look, but she turned away and kept going, rebuttoning her blouse all the way to her neck.

Sneaking past the other uniformed cops was easy. Once you got this far, everyone figured you belonged. She saw the reporters still complaining and pleading for a story, knocking against each other like pigs in a chute. She smiled and climbed up on the pier.

The focus of everyone's attention seemed to be the Coast Guard cutter at the end of the pier. Uniforms and plainclothes milled around in front of it, but no one went aboard. She saw Lt. Green talking to a couple of guys in dark suits and sunglasses. Harmon and Leeds from the FBI. Who else would be dumb enough to wear dark suits in 78° Miami heat. They were all obviously waiting for somebody. Him, the guy walking down the pier. The three men went over to meet this new guy. He wore expensive sunglasses, tinted a slightly reddish color. His hair was slicked back *GO*-style. His suit was lightweight and fashionable. Eight hundred bucks at least. He marched right by the three men, talking to them as he did. They fell in beside him.

She ducked behind the fender of an ambulance, slipped the Nikon from her purse, and snapped a few shots of the men. Then she headed for the Coast Guard cutter.

There were two cops at the gangplank.

"Lt. Green on board?" she asked.

"No," one of them answered.

"Tell him I'll wait for him below deck." She patted her purse. "We don't want the chemicals he asked for out in the sun. Last time that happened he chewed my butt out pretty bad."

One of the cops chuckled at that. "Yeah. I've got a few toothmarks myself. We'll tell him."

She hurried up the gangplank. Once on deck, she looked around, but there was nothing unusual. As soon as she went below deck she pulled out the camera again and began snapping everything she saw. So far, nothing looked out of place.

Until she stepped into the galley.

Her throat immediately contracted, as if it didn't want the same air that was in this room. Her stomach lurched, recalling the shrimp salad she'd had for lunch. She forced herself to relax, take deep breaths. Concentrate on the camera, the photographs.

She raised the camera to her right eye and pressed the shutter button.

The twenty dead men on the floor didn't mind. They were bound and gagged, five of them in their underwear, uniforms missing. All had bullet holes through their heads, execution-style. Fat black flies were buzzing around the room in giddy circles. Occasionally they would land and nibble at someone's wound.

She swallowed and snapped another picture.

Suddenly a large arm wrapped around her waist, pulling her backwards out of the room. A hand snatched her camera away.

"You know better, Dahlia," Lt. Green said, releasing her, but keeping the camera.

"C'mon, Lieutenant. Give a working girl a break."

Lt. Green opened the back of the camera and exposed the film. "That line ever work, Dahlia?"

She grinned. "Sometimes. If they're young enough and I'm wearing that skirt with the slit up to here." She tapped her thigh.

"Yeah, I know the one. My favorite."

"Why, Lieutenant"—she smiled—"you dirty old man."

He handed her back the exposed film.

She sighed. "Do any good to mention the First Amendment?"

"You'll have to wait for an official statement like all the other reporters." He guided her out of the galley. The two FBI guys and the third man, the one in charge, were waiting in the hall. "She took pictures," Lt. Green told them.

"Hi, Leeds. Hi, Harmon." She waved at the agents.

15

"How's tricks at the FBI. You two earn your wiretapping merit badges yet?"

The man in the expensive suit and tinted sunglasses frowned. "Who is this bimbo?"

"Bimbo!" she hollered. "Listen, asshole—"

Lt. Green stepped between them. "Whoa! Hold on here." He turned to the man. "This is Dahlia McGuire. Reporter out of the *Herald*. She's a pain in the ass, but she's fair. Most of the time I'd just as soon throw her skinny butt in jail as give her the time of day, but I won't have you coming around her badmouthing her. You want to work with me, fine. I've got orders to cooperate. But once, you've finished up here and blown back to where you came from, we'll still have to live here and work with these people. So you show some respect. Got me?"

The man in the suit stared at Lt. Green, then at Harmon and Leeds. Their blank expressions showed they agreed with Lt. Green. The man in the suit nodded curtly, turned, and climbed back up on the deck. The two agents followed.

"Hey, thanks, Lieutenant," Dahlia McGuire said. "That was nice. So what's going on here? Who killed these guys? Where are the uniforms? Some kind of drug deal? And what's the scoop on the pretty boy in the suit? CIA?"

Lt. Green scowled at her. "Shut up, McGuire."

She followed him up the stairs to the deck. When they got there, the guy in the suit whispered something to Lt. Green. He nodded.

"Wait down there, McGuire," the lieutenant said.

"What for?" she demanded.

"For questioning. After all, you are trespassing on government property. I'm going to have to hold you for questioning."

"Come on, Lieutenant. That's a crock and you know it."

Lt. Green smiled. "Right now it's for questioning. You wanna try for arrest?"

Dahlia McGuire swore under her breath and stomped back down the stairs. As soon as she heard the door slam behind her, she tiptoed back up the stairs and pressed her ear to the door. She could barely hear what they were saying.

"What do you make of it, gentlemen?" the guy in the suit was asking.

"Maybe just drugs," Agent Harmon said.

Lt. Green snorted. "No way. This was planned too well. Sure, drugs may be involved, but I think there's more to it, a bigger score down the line. Too many small signs. Plus, you wouldn't be here if you didn't know something you're not telling us."

There was a pause, and Dahlia shifted her ear for better hearing.

"What do you think, Adams?" Agent Leeds finally asked.

The man in the suit sighed. "Lt. Green is correct. There is something more going on. But I can't tell you what yet."

"Terrific," Lt. Green said. "We gotta work in the dark on this while you guys at Langley play your cards close to the vest. Terrific."

"No choice, Lieutenant. National security."

"That phrase has lost some credibility lately, pal."

"Nevertheless, that's our position," Adams said.

"What now?" Lt. Green asked.

"The three of you continue your investigation as you

would with any other case. Meantime, I'll call in a specialist.''

"A what?''

"Someone who knows how to deal with the kind of people who would do something like this. Unofficially.''

"Unofficially go after a bunch of killers. You know someone like that, huh?''

Adams hesitated. When he spoke, Dahlia thought his voice sounded grim. "Maybe. Just maybe.''

3

Matt Hunter piloted the airboat across the marshy saw grass, squinting against the sun for some sign of John Eagle. The old Seminole was always doing this to him, giving him these mysterious Indian directions, half in the Seminole Muskogean language, and then expecting Hunter to show up on time. A little game they played.

Hunter eased the airboat up to the small island, what the locals called a hammock, and cut the engine. He stepped onto the empty wooden cage and looked around. Cupping his hands around his mouth, he called, "John. John Eagle."

No answer. Of course, John Eagle was not his friend's real name. The truth had come out during a particularly intense drinking bout one evening last year at John Eagle's home. They had both pretended to be drunker than they were. Somehow it made talking easier. John had been enraged. His mother was a full-blooded Seminole, he'd said, descended from a Creek Indian chief. But his father was only half Seminole. The other half was Irish. John

Eagle's real name, he'd thundered angrily, was John *Finnegan*. "John Eagle," he'd explained, "is my spiritual name."

Hunter stood atop the cage and smiled at the memory. It didn't matter to him. After all, Hunter wasn't his real name either. Nor was Matt. But the reasons for his change were a little harder to explain. So he never did.

Over to the left the brush rustled. By the cypress trees. Something was moving fast. Coming toward him.

"John. That you?"

The tops of the brush wavered as something big trampled everything in its way.

Hunter hefted an old surplus knapsack on his back and grabbed the neatly coiled rope from atop the cage. He hopped ashore, first testing to make sure the land was solid. In the Everglades, even the land could fool you.

The rustling became louder. He could barely see the shape of a man running through the underbrush, almost to the clearing.

"John Eagle?"

"Who else?" John Eagle hollered as he burst into the clearing at a full gallop. He ran fast for a man in his sixties. But then he had to. A ten-foot alligator was running behind him, snapping at his heels.

Hunter laughed.

"What's so goddamn funny?" John panted, barely keeping ahead of the fat reptile. "The bastard thinks I'm Captain Hook or something."

"It's the hair," Hunter said, not moving to help. "They're attracted to gray hair."

"You should live so long to get hair this gray." John Eagle switched courses and ran straight for Hunter. The alligator followed.

"Shit!" Hunter said, dodging in the opposite direction.

"Ha! Not so goddamn funny now, huh white man?" John Eagle chuckled as he ran. The alligator stayed on the Seminole's tail, its clawed front feet moving together so that it ran with a slight rabbit hop. John was comfortably ahead, but when he glanced over his shoulder to check the reptile's progress, his foot hit a soft spot of peat and muck and his right leg sank up to the knees. He struggled to pull it free, twisting and yanking on it. No use. The alligator, low to the ground like some sleek Italian sports car, zoomed toward him, its jaws already yawning open. It hissed as it closed in on him.

"Luck of the Irish, eh John?" Hunter said, tossing his lasso over the alligator's open snout. He jerked hard on the rope, and the huge mouth slammed shut. The fat reptile forgot about John Eagle and began thrashing about, trying to shake the rope free.

"This Tonto crap is bullshit," John said, tugging at his leg. "From now on, I'll do the roping."

"Fine. Give me decent directions and this wouldn't happen." Hunter reached into his knapsack and pulled out two cans of beer. He tossed one to John Eagle. "None of this 'Turn right at the old Calusa village' stuff."

John Eagle smiled, opened his beer. "Everybody knows where that is."

"The Calusa Indians disappeared by 1800. There *is* no village site."

"Yeah, but everybody knows where it *was*." He stopped pulling on his leg and took a long swallow of beer. "You did just fine. You're here, aren't you?"

"Barely."

John gestured at his immobile leg. "You going to give me a hand here?"

"I'll think about it." Hunter walked over to the still-thrashing alligator. Its black horny plates glistened like shiny armor under the bright Florida sun. It grunted with each jerk of its neck. Frustrated, it lashed its heavy tail around at Hunter's feet. He hopped out of the way just in time. "He's a tough one. Ought to be worth four, maybe five hundred."

John Eagle drained the last of his beer, crushed the can, and slipped it into his pocket. He pointed to Hunter's unopened can. "If you're not going to drink that—"

"Jesus!" Hunter said as the alligator's long jaws snapped apart the heavy rope. It lifted its head and let out a deep loud roar, then charged straight for Hunter. Hunter jumped out of the way and the alligator spotted John Eagle, still stuck in the peat. "One beer coming up," Hunter said and threw the can to John.

John Eagle shook the can vigorously as the alligator ran at him. When it was within a few feet, he aimed the top of the can at the reptile's head and popped the tab. Beer sprayed into the alligator's eyes and nose. It stopped, shook its snout, blinked rapidly, then charged again.

"Geronimo," Hunter yelled, shucking his knapsack and leaping on the alligator's back.

"Geronimo?" John Eagle spat, pulling at his leg. "Fuck Geronimo. You're down here in Seminole country, buster, you yell 'Osceola!' "

"Sorry," Hunter said, holding on tightly as the alligator whipped its muscular body back and forth. Hunter pressed his knees into the reptile's sides, locking his arm under its neck. The alligator's tail snaked around and whacked him in the thigh. He felt as if someone had just hit him with a baseball bat.

"Sorry ain't enough, Hunter." John's leg was almost

free now. "There are only two hundred Seminoles left in the Everglades. But once, man, we owned this place. Osceola wiped out over two thousand U.S. soldiers back in the Second Seminole War. We cost the government sixty million dollars. And then they only captured Osceola during a parley under a goddamn flag of truce. Typical."

The scaly tail whipped around and smacked Hunter's thigh again. His leg went numb and lost its grip. He started slipping to the side, his left leg wedging under the belly of the alligator. A thick clawed foot the size of a softball dug into his calf. Pain jangled his brain, loosening his armlock around the alligator's neck.

"Even then we weren't finished," John Eagle continued complaining, ignoring Hunter's grunts and groans. "They had to pay us to leave Florida and go out to goddamn Oklahoma. Oklahoma, for Chrissake."

Hunter pulled himself back on top of the alligator, hooking his right leg under its belly. He dug the heel of his cowboy boot into its ribs and, using his armlock around its neck for leverage, began pulling back on the big head.

Finally he flipped the reptile over onto its back. Its stubby legs paddled helplessly in the air. Hunter straddled its broad white chest and clamped both hands around its snout. He held the jaws shut, his knuckles white against the pressure.

John Eagle pulled his foot all the way out of the sludge and looked over at Hunter. "I mean, what the hell's in Oklahoma?"

"The corn is as high as an elephant's eye," Hunter said, struggling to keep the alligator's jaws shut. "Think you could give me a hand here?"

John limped over to Hunter's discarded knapsack, shaking

23

the mud from his leg as he walked. He rooted through the pack, found the heavy-gauge steel wire, and walked over to Hunter. Quickly, expertly, he looped the wire around the alligator's jaws.

Hunter stood up. His whole body was splattered with mud and slime. Blood streaked down his ankle where his pants were torn. He looked exhausted.

John Eagle picked up the can of beer he'd squirted into the alligator's eyes and shook it. A little splashed around inside. He tossed it to Hunter. "You look like you could use this."

Hunter finished what was left of the can, crushed it, and stuck it in his knapsack. He nodded toward the subdued alligator. "This the way your grandfather used to do it?"

John Eagle snorted. "Closest my grandfather got to one of these was opening his alligator-leather wallet to buy moonshine."

"Which grandfather? The Indian or the Irish?"

John shrugged. "Both."

"Here he comes," Hunter said, pointing at the airboat zipping toward them. They were standing on Hunter's porch.

"How do you want to do this?" John Eagle asked.

"Straightforward."

"No, no, never work. We could do good guy, bad guy. You up to some snarling and foaming at the mouth?"

"Too hot to foam."

"How about dumb and stubborn Cajun? You want to do that?"

Hunter shook his head. "Too hard to do the accent."

John Eagle frowned at Hunter. "We can't insult the man. We gotta try something. It's expected."

Hunter finished his beer and started for the kitchen. "You want another?"

"You're still too white for this part of the business, Hunter. You don't understand the Indian mentality. The traditions."

"I understand enough. This is like Busk."

"Busk? What's that?"

"That's the ancient Seminole summer green-corn harvest ceremony. The Seminoles, the Creeks, and the Yuchis had the most intricate dance pattern of all the tribes. They performed in huge spirals, sometimes four spirals going at the same time. What you're about to do, it's the same thing."

John Eagle stared at Hunter with soft dark eyes. "Busk, huh? Where'd you learn about that?"

Hunter shrugged. "Here and there."

"You're part Indian, aren't you? I mean, forget the blond hair and pale skin, a Swede in the woodpile maybe. Deep down you've got Indian blood. Am I right?"

Hunter smiled. "Another beer?"

John Eagle nodded.

The airboat pulled up to the dock between Hunter's and John Eagle's boats. A huge Seminole with long black hair hanging down his back climbed out of it. He wore a tight orange T-shirt with black lettering across his broad chest: LITTLE HAWK'S LIVE ALLIGATOR WRESTLING—DIXIE HIGHWAY, MIAMI. His painter's cap proclaimed: LITTLE HAWK'S CAFE AND SOUVENIR SHOP. And the side of his airboat read: LITTLE HAWK'S EVERGLADES TOURS.

Clark Little Hawk walked across the dock to the ten-foot alligator in the wooden crate. He stooped down, examining the reptile from all angles, frowning and shaking his head a lot.

25

"Look at the son of a bitch act," John Eagle whispered to Hunter. They stood above the dock on Hunter's porch. The house itself was a modified *chikee*, the traditional Seminole home built on a stilted platform above the water. Hunter's house had the same log framework and thatched roof that John Eagle's Indian ancestors' had. But Hunter had added a couple of refinements. Like walls. And a porch.

"Hey, Clark Little Hawk." Hunter waved as the Indian climbed onto the porch. "You want a beer?"

Little Hawk patted his ample belly. "Got any Perrier?"

"Perrier?" John Eagle groused. "You're a Seminole, not a Yuppie."

"I think I've got some from the last time you were here," Hunter said and went into the house. He grabbed two beers and a Perrier from the small refrigerator that the generator kept running. On the way through the living room, he popped a tape into his portable cassette player. By the time he was back on the porch, the soundtrack from *Oklahoma!* could be heard.

"Very funny," John Eagle said to him, taking the beer.

"You got *Annie*?" Clark Little Hawk asked. "That one knocks me out."

"Sorry," Hunter said, handing him the Perrier.

The small bottle disappeared in Clark Little Hawk's giant hand. Little Hawk was in his mid-thirties, owner of half a dozen businesses in the area, renowned for fists as tight as they were large.

Hunter stood between the two big Seminoles and quietly sipped his beer. Hunter was not an especially tall man, but people talking to him almost always got the impression that they were looking up at him. There was something in his stance, a looseness maybe, that exuded confidence. His voice was quiet, almost gentle, but those he spoke to always heard every word. They made a point of it. However, this kind of talking was the specialty of John Eagle and Clark Little Hawk, more a form of entertainment than anything else.

The alligator let out another loud roar.

"Big mother, huh?" John Eagle said.

Clark Little Hawk looked back down at the crate as if he'd already forgotten about the alligator. "Him?"

"Who else?"

"Yeah, he's big enough, but he don't sound so good."

"What do you want him to do? Sing 'Stormy Weather'?"

"You know what I mean. Maybe he's sick."

"Sick my ass, Little Hawk."

"I just don't want no sick 'gator. They move too slow, don't put on a good show for the tourists."

"Slow? You want to see how slow he moves, go down and open that cage. You'll have all the slow you can handle."

Little Hawk shrugged. "How much?"

"Six hundred."

"Where's the other one?"

"What other one?" John Eagle asked.

"Hell, for six hundred I figured there were two of them."

Hunter chuckled.

"I'll tell you what, John Eagle: I'll give you three hundred."

"Three hundred?"

"Business has been going to hell lately. Tourists don't wanna watch a fat Indian wrassle an alligator. They wanna go to Disney World, see Mickey Mouse."

"You've been telling me that for six years. Five hundred."

"Four fifty."

"Look at this." John Eagle tugged up Hunter's pant leg, revealing the bandaged wound. "That scaly bastard almost killed my partner."

"Where were you?"

John Eagle sighed. "Okay, four fifty. But you load him yourself."

Little Hawk counted out the cash, squeezing each bill as it left his hand.

"Come on, Little Hawk," Hunter said. "I'll help you load up."

"Thanks, Hunter."

The three of them loaded the crate onto Little Hawk's airboat and watched him roar away. John Eagle shook his head as Little Hawk disappeared amongst the saw grass. "If he wasn't my nephew, I'd have held out for more."

"If he wasn't your nephew, he'd have only paid four hundred."

John Eagle gave Hunter his half of the money and climbed into his own airboat. "Why don't you come on over tonight? Got some fresh ones." He reached down into the boat and held up a large jar. Eight fat frogs kicked furiously against each other. "Fried or barbequed, your choice."

Hunter shook his head. "One more frog and I'll start catching flies with my tongue. Thanks anyway."

"See you tomorrow." John Eagle waved.

"Right. Only let's meet here first. Save us both some time."

John Eagle laughed as he sped away.

*   *   *

Adams paddled the canoe through the dark swamp water as silently as he had once done in Vietnam. Of course, now he wore a linen suit and fancy silk tie, but he didn't mind. Even in this heat. To him it was just another kind of uniform, another kind of war. The enemy was the same.

Under his left arm, his Beretta 92SB hugged his ribs. That hadn't changed either.

The bright Florida moon made navigation easy. Occasionally he'd hear a slurping sound as a fat alligator slid down a muddy embankment into the water to investigate. One alligator swam too close to the canoe and Adams bonked it on the head with his paddle. It hissed at him, turned, and swam away.

"Yer mamma," Adams said and kept paddling.

Up ahead, through the saw grass, the palms, the cypresses, and the saw palmettos, he spotted Matt Hunter's house. The evening fog swirled around the stilted platform, making the house look as if it were hovering above clouds, like some castle inhabited by Norse gods.

Adams grimaced. Hunter was no god, no saint. Not even an agent anymore. That made him fair game.

A mosquito landed on Adams's wrist. Adams stopped paddling and watched the spidery insect drink his blood, its leg bowing slightly with each slurp. He reached out and brushed it away.

He paddled up to Hunter's dock. There were no lights on in the house, but Hunter's airboat was tied up. Adams climbed out of the canoe without making a sound. He unsnapped the safety strap from his holster and pulled out the Beretta. Slowly, soundlessly, he walked around the porch, peeking into the dark windows. The overhanging trees shaded the house from the moon, so he couldn't see anything inside. Just darkness.

He clamped his hand on the door handle. There was no lock. Gently he nudged the door inward.

A board creaked above him.

He spun around, the Beretta in front of him. But Hunter was already in motion, swinging down from the roof, feet thumping Adams in the chest, knocking him backwards into the house. The Beretta flew against the wall as Adams sprawled onto his back. For a fraction of a second, Adams saw Hunter framed in the doorway, the night fog aglow with dim fluorescence from the moon as it curled around him. He was faceless in the dark. Faceless, compassionless, a trained assassin. For the first time in years, Adams felt fear.

But Hunter did not move toward Adams. He remained in the doorway. "The answer is no."

Adams sat up. "You haven't heard the offer."

Hunter walked over to Adams's Beretta, picked it up, examined it. "Still carrying this?"

"You gave it to me."

Hunter tossed the gun to Adams. "Sentiment could get you killed."

Adams slipped the Beretta back into its holster. "I couldn't be sure you were still alive. They might have already gotten to you."

"Who?"

"Got a beer?"

Hunter stared at Adams a moment, then nodded. "There's a lamp over there. Got a match?"

"I'm an agent, Hunter, not a Boy Scout."

"Here." Hunter lobbed a Bic lighter at Adams, then disappeared into the kitchen.

Adams felt his way blindly to the kerosene lamp, finally lighting it. He held the lamp up and looked around the room. "Jesus," he whistled. There was only one room, the kitchen separated by a brightly colored Indian blanket hanging from the ceiling to the floor. The rest of the room was rustic but comfortable: wood-burning stove, over-stuffed couch and chair, guitar on the wall, and lots of books piled around, some open and marked with a wooden match or a feather.

One of Adams's driving obsessions back when he'd worked with Hunter was finding out the man's true identity. Hunter had come from the service, where his real records had been filed "Top Secret" by some general. No one knew Hunter's real name or where he came from. Adams had been compiling a private file on him for years, running down leads, trying to find out more. Competely unofficial, like a hobby. But more than that too.

Hunter reappeared, carrying a can of beer and a glass of apple juice. He handed the beer to Adams. It was an obscure Chinese beer that Adams had developed a fondness for on one of their assignments. You couldn't get it in the United States.

"You hate this brand," Adams said.

"I've been saving it for you. I knew you'd show up again sooner or later."

Adams sat on the couch. "Nice place. Looks like a commune or something, like from the sixties."

"Don't knock communes. They can be a lot of fun."

Adams raised an eyebrow. "*You* lived on a commune?"

Hunter smiled.

Adams filed the information away. The FBI had done a lot of intelligence gathering on communes. Maybe when he got back he could go through the files, dig something up. "Anyway, it's nice here. Quiet. Still play guitar, huh?"

"Now and then."

"No paintings, though, just blankets."

"Just blankets."

"You like Indian blankets, huh?"

"I like the bright-colored stripes. They did that in imitation of the brocaded materials worn by the Spanish."

Adams wondered if Hunter was toying with him now. Hunter knew about Adams's file. Hell, Adams had told him himself.

"Listen, Matt, you know I wouldn't have come here if I didn't think it was important."

"It's always important."

"We're serious about this one."

"You people are always serious."

"Don't give me that 'you people' shit, Hunter," Adams said angrily. "You were one of us for a long time. And you were the best."

Hunter drained his apple juice and smiled. "Still am the best, kid. But I'm no longer one of you. I'm an entrepreneur now. Got my own business."

"Catching goddamn alligators? That's your hotshot business?"

"Hey, don't put down alligators. They're not only the last living link with dinosaurs, but they're the nearest living relatives of the birds. Has something to do with the evolution of their forelegs."

Adams felt a headache coming on. The one he always got when dealing with Hunter. He called them "Hunter migraines." "Where do you pick up that stuff?"

Hunter shrugged. "Here and there."

"Yeah, well, let's get down to the here and now. I'm not just talking about an assignment for old times' sake.

I'm talking about saving your own worthless life too." He took a deep breath. "We think Rostov's in the country."

Hunter stared directly into Adams's eyes. The flickering light from the kerosene lamp washed out the pupils, leaving only two staring disks of icy blue. Hunter started for the door.

"Where you going?" Adams asked, standing.

"You should have let me kill him when I had the chance."

"We were under orders, damm it. We needed him to trade for one of our own. You know that."

Hunter marched down the dock and climbed into his airboat.

Adams ran after him. "Come on, Matt. You know if Rostov is here it means something big. He's the baddest fucking terrorist in the world."

Hunter started the airboat. "He's your problem now." He revved the motor and banked the boat sharply, sending a spray of water back over Adams's linen suit and fancy silk tie.

4

The cabdriver pulled up to the curb, crunching the empty beer cans, plastic Big Mac cartons, and the rest of the garbage jammed against the curb. He snapped the meter flag off and turned around to face his fare. Once again he looked admiringly at the tall man's expensive gray suit, obviously hand-tailored, the shiny maroon tie, gleaming white shirt, gold tie pin.

"You sure this is the place you want?" the cabby asked.

"This the Ponce de León Hotel, no?" Rostov said in Spanish.

"*Sí*, this is what you asked for. You wish me to wait?"

"No. How much do I owe you?"

"Seven dollars and fifty cents."

Rostov handed him a ten-dollar bill. "Keep it."

"Thank you, *señor*."

Rostov climbed out of the cab, clutching the duffel bag in his left hand, and looked up at the Ponce de León Hotel.

Perhaps once, forty or fifty years ago, it had been a showplace, *the* hotel to stay in while visiting Miami, or to meet that special someone for a high-class rendezvous. Not anymore. Now it looked as if it had been dipped in grime, rolled in grease, then dropped back on this block from a great height. The whole building seemed to lean to the right.

Rostov walked into the lobby. The carpeting was colorless, but not odorless: the stench of something rotting mixed with stale cigarette smoke and a bitter underlying smell of urine.

The hotel manager looked up from his chair behind the counter. He was twenty pounds lighter than skinny, wearing a white golf shirt buttoned up to his scrawny neck. He munched on peanut butter and cheese crackers, licking some orange crumbs from his fingers. "You lost, pal?"

Rostov walked past him. "Thank you, but I can find it myself."

"Yeah, right. If not, we got plenty of peple in this place who'll help you find it." He snorted loudly at his joke and bit into another cracker.

Rostov looked at the rickety elevator and decided to take the stairs instead. It was only four flights. In Moscow he had to climb six flights most days because the elevator in his apartment building was always breaking down.

The people he passed on the stairs always looked at the duffel bag first, their dim eyes brightening at the possibilities of what might be inside, and what it might mean for them. Then they looked at the man, Rostov, and wondered why such an obviously well-off and handsome gentleman was strolling through the Ponce de León Hotel with a duffel bag. That's when their eyes would dim again, squint into their normal cynical sneer. They'd seen all kinds down here. Probably had some leather outfit in the bag, chains, a cattle prod. They'd shrug knowingly and move on.

Rostov reached the fourth floor just as a door burst open and a chubby bald man ran out. A naked Latin girl, maybe seventeen, stood in the doorway and threw a shoe at him.

"From behind," she complained in Spanish, "that is ten dollars extra."

"Bullshit," the fat man drawled, jamming a cowboy hat on his bald head. "Where I come from it don't matter which door you go in, the price is the same."

He spun around and bumped into Rostov. "Watch it, partner," he said and started to pass by.

Rostov grabbed the man by the throat with a pincer hold, his thumb and fingers almost meeting behind the fat man's jugular. He felt the man's pulse thumping wildly beneath the fingertips as he shoved him against the wall. When Rostov spoke, his voice was calm, but the fiery eyes displayed a terrible anger. "You must be more careful. Watch where you are going."

The fat man gagged and clawed at Rostov's powerful grip. Rostov snapped his wrist, and the fat man's eyes rolled up in his head and he dropped to the floor unconscious. Rostov absently tugged on the cuff of his left sleeve and continued down the hall, ignoring the naked young girl standing unashamed in the doorway.

As soon as Rostov passed her door, the naked girl dashed out, went through the fat cowboy's pockets, emptied his wallet of cash and credit cards, and hurried back into her room, bolting the door behind her.

Rostov knocked at Room 412.

"Yeah?" the voice inside called in an unfriendly tone.

"Special delivery," Rostov said.

The door opened, and three burly men stood in the doorway with guns. One of them was black; the other two were white. None weighed less than two hundred pounds; none was older than twenty-two.

"That you, buddy?" the voice behind them called. "Let him in, guys. Get the fucking show on the road."

The three men stepped aside and allowed Rostov to enter. Rostov took in the room without seeming to even notice it. He noted exits, how many feet to the windows, the location of the bathroom. If asked, he could have sat down and drawn a blueprint of the room as exact as the original architect's.

Mickey Seidman was lying down on the bed, his shoes and socks off, an elegantly dressed woman rubbing his feet. Mickey was dressed casually: blue crew-neck shirt, pleated gabardine pants, beige shoes, nubby cotton sports jacket, diamond stud in his left earlobe. Rostov calculated that the outfit was worth a little more than a thousand dollars. Mickey was only twenty-three years old.

"Sit down, man." Mickey gestured at the other twin bed. "This here is Tina."

"How do you do?" Rostov said, sitting.

The woman looked up. Despite her expensive and youthful clothing, Rostov could see the slight signs of age on her face beneath the makeup. She was probably thirty-five or so. She was also stoned.

"Dig this, man," Mickey said, sitting up. "I been doing this shit for a few years now, making a fuck of a lot of money, buying the fancy clothes and cars and all that kind of shit. Thing is, man, I get together with the other assholes with money, you know, socialize and stuff. Only these other guys I see, well they got their money more or less legit, fucking the people who buy their products rather than the junkies and hoods we deal with. Only difference I can figure out is that they can advertise on the goddamn *Tonight Show* and I can't. I mean, you picture ole Johnny Carson holding up a Baggie of blow, taking a snort on the air, and sayin', 'Best shit I ever had'?''

Rostov looked at his watch. ''Could we conduct our business now?''

''Yeah, yeah, right. Thing is, I figure, hey, I gotta live with these rich assholes now, fuckin' their daughters and such, so I might as well learn how to talk to the old farts. So I start takin' like evenin' classes at the community college. English and stuff. Tina here was my teacher.''

Tina smiled, then dropped the smile as if she couldn't remember what was so funny in the first place.

''So it turns out Tina here's been living this goody-goody Catholic life her whole fuckin' life and is ready for a little walk on the wild side. A month later she's suckin' off every guy in here and snortin' a hundred bucks a day. You dig it? Hell, she'll even do you right now if you whip it out. Right, hon?''

Tina smiled. ''Yeah, sure.''

''Maybe later.'' Rostov unzipped the duffel bag and pulled out a Baggie of cocaine. He handed it to Mickey.

Mickey pulled a black telephone into his lap and dialed. The other party answered immediately. ''Yeah, man, it's me. Put the foreign dude on the phone.'' Pause. ''Yeah, he's right here. Hold on.'' Mickey handed Rostov the receiver. ''Your buy.''

Rostov spoke into the phone. ''Nikko? . . . Yes, everything here is okay. Do they have all the weapons? The grenades? . . . Good. How many crates? . . . Yes, that's enough. What about the rocket launchers and the plastic

explosives?'' He listened, nodding, then turned to Mickey.
''You are two crates short of Uzis.''

Mickey shrugged. ''My supplier jerked me off, man. I
made up for it with an extra case of bazookas.''

Rostov spoke into the phone. ''Did you hear that? Yes,
that will do.'' He handed the phone back to Mickey.

''Nikko, baby, put Banning back on. Banning? Hold
on.'' Mickey snapped his fingers at the three hulking
bodyguards. ''Okay, guys, everything's cool. Go wait in
the hall, keep an eye out for cops.''

The three men left.

Mickey tore open the bag, dipped his finger in, and
tasted the powder. He smiled and sang, ''Rock and roll is
here to stay, it will never die.'' Quickly he jumped to his
feet, grabbed a mirror from the dresser, dumped some
cocaine from the bag onto it, and handed the whole thing
to Tina. ''Go for it, babe.''

Tina rooted through her purse, pulled out a gold razor
blade and straw. She tucked her baby-fine blond hair
behind her ears and leaned over the mirror. With the
concentration of a diamond cutter, she separated a six-inch
line from the pile. The lining of her right nostril was raw
and sore, so she stuck the gold straw into her left nostril
and pinched the right one closed with her thumb. She
inhaled, following the line of coke like an aardvark tracing
a line of ants.

Mickey spoke into the phone. ''Yeah, it's good. Let
'em have the weapons.'' He hung up and held out his hand
to Rostov. ''Pleasure doin' business with you, man.''

Rostov smiled. ''The pleasure is all mine.'' His right
hand lashed out, his open palm striking Tina on the back
of her head, driving the gold straw up her nose.

''Mickey!'' she screamed, lifting her head. The straw

stuck out of the end of her nose, blood funneling down and streaming out the end as if it were a faucet.

Not giving Mickey a chance to react, Rostov grabbed him by the throat and ran him up against the wall with a loud thud. Mickey sagged slightly, dazed. The door began to open. Rostov yanked the .45 from Mickey's belt and fired five shots through the door. Slowly the door swung open to reveal one of Mickey's bodyguards slumped on the ground, his big fist still clutching the doorknob. The other two bodyguards were sprawled in a bleeding heap behind him.

Mickey revived enough to start struggling, prying at Rostov's fingers, chopping at his arm. Rostov smiled again. "Perhaps you want your gun back?" He jammed the .45 back into Mickey's belt and fired three times down into his crotch. Mickey's eyes went wild with agony. Then the lids closed and the body went limp. Rostov released his grip and Mickey crumpled to the floor, dead.

Tina was screaming frantically now, flapping her arms disorientedly. She managed to yank the gold straw free from her nostril, but the blood continued to pour down her lips, mouth, and chin.

"Silly woman," Rostov said, clucking his tongue. He grabbed a handful of her hair and hurled her forward through the dirty window. Glass exploded outward, and the jagged edges still stuck in the window raked her body as she sailed through, screaming as she plummeted to the sidewalk.

Rostov calmly surveyed his work and nodded with satisfaction. He tugged on his left sleeve, stepped over the bodies of Mickey's bodyguards, and walked out of the room. A breeze swept through the broken window and swirled the cocaine across the floor like so much chalk dust.

* * *

Mikal Rostov was drenched with sweat. He heard a whimpering sound, but was only vaguely aware that it came from him. His body felt as if it were encased in a tight rubber suit that kept shrinking. His limbs were numb, the sweat hot as boiling water, sizzling across his skin like butter in a skillet. It was the same nightmare. The same one, over and over. The one about Matt Hunter.

Africa. A new nation whose name was bigger than the country. The last stop for the U.S. Secretary of State on an anti-apartheid mission. It was a last-minute decision, the President ordering Secretary Jennings to pay a personal visit to the ailing Prime Minister Bhawoona. KGB had found out about the plans at great cost and immediately contacted Rostov.

Documents were fabricated, confessions prepared, evidence arranged. Secretary Jennings's death would be blamed on South African black rebels. The anti-apartheid cause would be set back another decade. The strife and violence would continue. And with the United States keeping its distance after Secretary Jennings' assassination, Moscow would have an easier time increasing its influence. The plan would work, as it had so often in so many other countries.

African security had been laughable. Not long out of the jungles and the sway of Christian missionaries, the armies were still sloppy, too trusting. Rostov had needed to kill only three men, boys really, to enter the prime minister's palace. Blood from one disemboweled young soldier freckled his boot. He wiped it off on the back of his leg and continued down the palace hallway, the green duffel bag slung over his shoulder.

He was climbing the wide marble stairway just as Secretary Jennings's motorcade arrived. There was much shouting and cheering outside. "The Star-Spangled Banner" was played on traditional African instruments.

From his perch on the balcony, Rostov could see the large doorway where Secretary Jennings would soon be entering the palace. Servants aligned themselves on each side of the door and stood at attention. The head servant fussed and fluttered about them, straightening their ties, brushing lint from their shoulders. Four purely decorative guards stood at attention, armed with only the traditional spears the Mugamba tribe had used to drive out their rivals two centuries ago.

The front door opened and Secretary Jennings and Prime Minister Bhawoona entered, the excited cheers of the crowd washing around them. They turned, waved one last time as the doors were closed. When the doors slammed shut, the prime minister sagged slightly, the effects of his age, eighty-three, and illness plain on his face. Secretary Jennings offered the prime minister his arm for support. Bhawoona smiled gratefully and took it.

How sweet, Rostov thought as he unzipped his duffel bag in the dark recesses of the balcony. It took him only seconds to remove and set up his M47 Dragon Medium Anti-Tank/Assault Weapon (MAW). Though not as effective or as portable as other MAWs or LAWs, like the Armbrust Disposable, the M47 Dragon had been specifically chosen because a shipment had been stolen from the manufacturer, McDonnel-Douglas Corporation, in St. Louis. The ammunition had been stolen from Raytheon Company in Bristol, Tennessee. Clues had been left identifying the anti-apartheid rebels as the thieves.

But the Dragon would do its job. Outfitted with sixty side-thruster solid-propellant motors, SACLOS guidance, thermal 390 W battery, and roll reference gyro, the Dragon could penetrate three feet of concrete.

Secretary Jennings and Prime Minister Bhawoona were coming straight toward Rostov now. Rostov checked his watch. Right on time. Of all his skills at assassination, torture, military coups, Rostov was most proud of his timing. He planned everything to the second. His black Swiss watch was his one extravagance. It had cost more than some small automobiles. But it had been with him on a hundred missions and never missed a second.

Now was no exception. The watch said it was time to fire within ten seconds. Ten seconds. A lifetime to the two men down there.

Rostov shouldered the Dragon and sighted Secretary Jennings through the x6 scope of the tracker. All Rostov had to do was fire the missile and afterwards keep the tracker crosshairs on Secretary Jennings's chest. An infrared detector in the tracker would pick up a signal from the IR transmitter in the tail of the missile and the thrusters would adjust automatically to hit whatever the tracker was focused on. It couldn't miss.

Rostov thumbed aside the safety. He squinted into the telescope: Secretary Jennings and Prime Minister Bhawoona were laughing at something. Rostov grinned, held his breath, and slowly began to tighten the trigger grip.

Suddenly he felt hard cold metal thump against his ear. He carefully lowered the MAW. He said the name before he even looked back: "Hunter."

"Aw, you ruined the surprise."

Rostov started to turn, but Hunter jammed the muzzle of his .45 into Rostov's ear. "Shhh."

They waited like that until Secretary Jennings and Prime Minister Bhawoona and their entourage had passed. When they finally were alone, Rostov turned with a snarl, "You must not—"

Hunter shoved the gun hard into Rostov's ear, ripping skin. "I said to be quiet. Maybe I should clean some of that ear wax out for you, Rostov." He thumbed back the hammer of his gun.

The click echoed loudly in Rostov's ear. He felt himself trembling, his bladder swelling. He had no choice but to try to escape. Foolishly he grabbed at Hunter's gun.

Immediately Hunter sidestepped the attempt and swung his elbow into Rostov's nose. Blood squirted out each nostril as the Russian fell back to the floor. Hunter leaped on top of his chest, straddling him, pressing the gun against his broken nose, leaning into it a little.

Hunter chuckled, but it was not an amused sound. It was more like a growl. "My orders say to bring you back alive. Seems the boys behind the desks think they can swap you for one of ours. I say any deal that lets you live is a lousy one. I'm tempted to kill you anyway." Hunter's blue eyes seemed paler, almost gray. Rostov didn't move. "But I'm thinking about our guy's wife and daughter waiting for him to come back. You know what a sentimental guy I am."

Rostov nodded. He had seen the damage Hunter could do. Had seen inpenetrable buildings looted of secret papers, piles of dead bodies left behind. All the work of one man. Hunter. The man with no past.

Hunter shifted his gun to his left hand and pulled a thick combat knife from his boot. "I want you to remember this moment, Rostov. And since I don't have a camera, I'll have to improvise." He pulled Rostov's left arm away from his body and pinned it to the floor with his knee. He pulled up the sleeve, revealing Rostov's prized watch.

Rostov began to struggle, and Hunter whipped the pistol across his broken nose. Rostov stopped struggling.

Hunter stabbed the blade straight into the watch, shattering the crystal and the works. With a deft flip of his blade, he sliced off the watch band. Slowly, deliberately, he pressed the sharp blade against Rostov's wrist until blood welled up around the shiny metal. He plowed the knife through the skin.

"You bastard!" Rostov said.

"I've always had trouble making new friends." When Hunter was finished, he wiped his blade on Rostov's hair and stuck it back into his boot. "From now on, every time you check your watch, you'll know what time it is, Rostov. Time to die."

Rostov looked at the back of his wrist, saw the large bloody H carved there. But it wasn't just blood seeping out of the wound; there was something else, something moving. Then the wound peeled open and hundreds of white maggots emerged, crawling out of his wrist and over his arm, and leaving a slimy trail of blood as they covered his body.

He screamed.

As always.

And as always, he bolted up in his bed.

The door to his room opened and Nikko and Kurt burst in, guns at the ready.

"The dream?" Nikko asked.

Rostov stared at his wrist before answering. He saw the big white H, each line of the scar like a fat worm lying on his skin. Sweat beaded all around the scar. Rostov rubbed his wrist, tugged down the sleeve of his pajama shirt. "Yes, the dream."

Rostov reached over to the bedside table and grabbed

the bottle of vodka. He took a long deep swig. The dream was coming more often now, almost every night. Sometimes it even came during the day, while he was awake. He could never get a good sleep, never really rest. The scar on his wrist was like a tattoo. Another man's initial on his skin. This could not be tolerated. He took another swig of vodka. It didn't help. Nothing did.

"Tomorrow," he said. "Tomorrow we kill Hunter."

Nikko bristled. "Tomorrow we begin the main operation."

"Hunter first."

"It would mean coming out in the open. You would be risking everything."

Rostov rubbed his wrist. The sweat evaporating from his body chilled him. "We kill Hunter, then finish the operation."

"He is one man. Not even an agent anymore. He can do nothing."

"You know him only by reputation. I have seen his work."

Nikko shook his head. "Mikal, please. You are obsessed."

Rostov threw the bottle of vodka across the room. It smashed into the wall. "It will be done."

"At home, they will not tolerate it."

"They will have to, won't they?"

Nikko did not answer. He and Kurt left the room.

Rostov leaned back against his pillow. He did not close his eyes for fear the nightmare would return. But he didn't mind. By tomorrow Hunter would be dead, and with him, the dream.

5

Prince Charles handed Hunter a hunk of wood. Hunter examined it, turning it over in his hands. "Too small," he said and tossed it back on the ground. "We're gathering firewood, kid, not building a birdhouse."

Prince Charles shrugged. "I'm tired."

"Tired, huh?"

"Uncle Clark made me run tours the whole day yesterday. Tourists asking dumb questions for ten hours. Shit, I'd rather wrestle the alligators."

"Wait until you turn sixteen, okay?" Hunter pulled a fat cypress trunk along the ground. Prince Charles ran over and helped him lug the fallen tree to the clearing. Prince Charles wasn't his real name; Charles Riverbend was. John Eagle was his great-uncle and Clark Little Hawk was his uncle. At fifteen, Charles was tired of the swamp, tired of the Seminole traditions, and tired of being a kid. He wanted to move to California, take up surfing, and never again hear about the glorious Seminole history. His teenage cynicism about his Seminole heritage had prompted John Eagle to dub him Prince Charles. Hunter understood his restlessness; that's why Charles was always visiting him.

"I been thinking," Prince Charles said tentatively.

"About?"

"Taking off. Heading out on my own." He sucked in a deep breath.

"California?"

"Yup. Malibu."

"Malibu's nice. Not the best surfing though."

"You surfed?" Prince Charles's voice was gleeful.

"Some." Hunter dropped the tree trunk, walked over to the airboat, and reached into the Igloo cooler.

"We gonna celebrate with a beer?" Prince Charles asked hopefully.

Hunter tossed him a cold can. "Juice."

Prince Charles frowned at the can of apple juice, pulled the tab, and drank. "Don't try to talk me out of it, Matt. I've made up my mind."

"Which run you make yesterday?"

"The long one. Ninety-nine miles along the Wilderness Waterway, cutting up through Flamingo and Everglades City. A charter of these four insurance guys at some convention in Miami. Tomorrow they want to go down Shark River. Uncle Clark's busy with the restaurant, so I gotta take 'em."

Hunter drank a can of apple juice. "So you're going to California instead. Malibu."

"Yeah, right. I've been playing swamp Indian long enough."

Hunter nodded. "Families are tough to live with. Tougher to live without. It isn't until you can't see them again that

50

you realize that." He looked out over the water. "Hear that sound?"

"The bird?"

"Yes. What kind is it?"

"Heron, sounds like."

"Yeah, but what kind?"

"I dunno. I can't see it."

"You don't have to see it, Charles. That low-pitched croak. It's a great blue heron. They've got some out in California. Over there, flying above that tree. What's that?"

"Sparrow, I guess. Who cares?"

"It's a loggerhead shrike. They feed on insects and rodents, sometimes even on smaller birds. Here's the thing that's strange: they like to hang their prey on thorns or barbed-wire fences."

"Really?"

"Really. Look a little like mockingbirds, don't they? Except for that black mask."

The boy pointed to a brown bird at the edge of the water. "I know that one. Sounds like a cuckoo. It's a bittern."

"But what kind? American Bittern or Least Bittern?"

"What's the difference?"

Hunter picked up a shell, tossed it near the bird. Immediately it leaped into flight. "There. See the black tips of the wings?"

"Yeah."

"That makes it an American Bittern."

Hunter went back and hefted his chainsaw.

Prince Charles stared at him. "Where'd you learn all this, Matt?"

"Here and—"

"There. I know. I mean, did you grow up in a hick dump like this or was it some big city?"

"I lived in both, kid. Found out something strange, too."

"What?"

"They're both the same. You'll be surprised how much like this place Malibu is. Not in looks maybe, but in other ways."

"I'm still going. Talking about birds didn't change my mind."

"Didn't think it would. Thing is, Christmas is coming up in a couple of weeks and a couple of months after that is your birthday and a couple of months after that you'll have finished the school year."

"I don't care about school. It's so easy. I don't even study and I get mostly A's."

"Mostly, but not all. Anyway, if you can hold off on Malibu until then, I think I can contact an old buddy out in Los Angeles who might have room for you to stay for the summer. He's got two kids of his own, but he can always squeeze one more in. You could stay with him while you figure out what you want to do."

"What about Uncle John and Uncle Clark? Not to mention Mom." Charles's father had been killed in Vietnam during the evacuation of Saigon.

"I'll talk to them."

A flock of pie-billed grebes suddenly burst into the sky in the distance. Hunter looked up.

"How old are your friend's kids?" Charles asked. "Are they—"

"Shhh," Hunter said, still staring at the birds. He stood perfectly still, listening. Faintly, like the distant drone of a mosquito, he heard the sound of airboats. More than one, more than two. He turned to Charles. "Get in your boat and go home. Go by way of Lostman's River."

"That's ten miles out of my way."

"Just do it. And when you get home, call your Uncle John and tell him not to meet me this morning."

Charles looked at his watch. "He's probably already left by now."

"Damn!" Hunter grabbed the saw and tossed it into the airboat. They were on a hammock only half a mile from his house. But the boats were coming fast.

"Listen," Charles said. "Some boats coming."

"Go!" Hunter said, pushing the kid toward his boat. "Now!"

"Got some girls coming over, Matt?" Charles winked.

"Yeah, I'm throwing a little party. Not for minors. Now take off before I kick your butt into the water."

Charles laughed and jumped into his airboat. The giant fan on top of the boat whirled and the little craft took off, skimming across the saw grass and water. Hunter started his airboat and sped toward home. Now he could see the boats rocketing behind him only a quarter of a mile away. And in the lead boat, the tall blond figure of Rostov.

Rostov was shouldering a grenade launcher. Nikko knelt next to him, aiming a British-made LAW 80 rocket launcher.

Hunter caught glimpses of Tomas, Kurt, and Koyo in the other boats. He counted nine additional terrorists distributed throughout the four airboats. Fourteen men altogether.

"Dammit, Rostov," Hunter muttered. "I knew you were crazy, but not this crazy."

Hunter had weapons in the house. A few grenades, an H&K G-11 caseless assault rifle, a couple of other good-

53

ies. Enough to put up a damn good fight. But there was no way he would make it. He was going to have to run.

He was twenty yards from the dock, ready to swerve in the opposite direction, when he heard the first LAW missile screaming toward him. The water erupted two feet off starboard, rocking the airboat. Another explosion burst five feet ahead of the bow. Water and mud splattered Hunter. Saw grass fluttered about like green confetti.

Two more rounds screeched at him. The first blew up the dock. Splinters of wood showered Hunter, jabbed at his skin, lodged in his hair and clothing. The second missile hit the fan housing, blowing the back of the airboat into sizzling shrapnel. A chunk of twisted fan the size of a thumb buzzsawed across the back of Hunter's neck.

With the boat sinking, Hunter had no choice now but to go for the house and try to reach his weapons before they blew him up too. He dove into the fresh water, felt the saw grass's serated blades slice through the skin on the backs of his hands. He swam underwater, his powerful legs kicking him closer to the shattered dock. A few feet away a grenade exploded in the water. The concussion sent a thick wave pushing at him like a giant fist. The sound of the explosion, magnified underwater, stabbed at his eardrums. He kept swimming.

Hunter pulled himself up onto the shattered dock, avoiding the jagged points of woods. The dock looked as if some swamp monster had taken a bite out of it.

He scrambled to his feet as the four airboats pulled into a tight formation less than two hundred yards in front of the house. He didn't have to look to know what they were doing. The four boats would be idling in a row. Each man would be raising his weapon now, waiting for Rostov's command. Rostov would be rubbing his wrist, touching the scar next to his watch, smiling, his insane eyes burning.

Hunter kept running. His wet shoes slipped a little on the wood, but he kept his balance and ran for the door.

A screaming whistle and the door exploded in front of him.

Hunter ran straight through the hole where the door had been, through the smoke, into the house.

Suddenly all fourteen men began firing at once. The clatter of machine guns, the booming of shotguns, the explosions of LAW missiles and grenades melded into one gruesome symphony of destruction as the house exploded in a dozen different places at once.

Rostov waved his men forward. The four boats slowly nosed through the water, approaching the smoking house with caution.

"He is dead," Nikko said. "Now we must get back."

"First, we find the body."

"He is dead!" Nikko repeated. "Look!"

Rostov stared at the ruins of the house, the collapsed walls, the debris floating in the swamp water. They drifted past a half-burned Indian blanket. A couple of empty beer cans floated by. "Find the body," Rostov said quietly.

They pulled up to the dock remains and Rostov and Nikko climbed out.

Rostov pointed at the pilot. "Take the boat over there and sift through the debris. Whatever moves, shoot."

The terrorist nodded and guided the boat away.

"Koyo, you come with us. You men too."

Koyo and three other terrorists emptied the fourth boat. Koyo tied it to the dock and ordered one of the men to stand guard.

Rostov turned to Kurt. "Kurt, you take the boat over by that hammock. It is the closest land. If he's alive, he will have to go there. Tomas, take your boat over that way." He pointed to the right side of the house. "Look through everything in the water. Everything."

"There are crocodiles here," Tomas said nervously.

"Then you open their mouths and look inside. Now go."

Tomas urged his boat through the murky water, the two terrorists with him poking their rifle butts at everything they passed.

Rostov led Nikko and Koyo up the ramp to the house. Rostov's pace was lively, anxious. He hoped to find Hunter inside, barely alive, just enough to feel the excruciating pain that Rostov would provoke.

He stepped across the smoldering doorway into the rubble of the house. Two walls were half blown away. The roof had collapsed on that side of the house. Bullet holes that had penetrated the wall allowed bright sunbeams to poke through like dozens of thin lasers. One of the stilts supporting the house had been damaged, and the whole structure listed to one side.

Rostov kicked through the debris as he walked. An old wooden chest with hand-carved borders lay on its side, the contents spilling out: a G-11 assault rifle, now shattered beyond use; a Detonics .45 Combat Master Mark IV, the barrel twisted; a few undetonated Misar MU 50-G hand grenades.

Rostov used his foot to poke through a pile of cassette tapes. He read the labels, trying to match the performers with some mental image of Matt Hunter: Bob Dylan, Linda Ronstadt, Willie Nelson, Nat King Cole, Tschaikovsky's *Symphony No. 5 in E Minor, Op. 64*, Bartok's

Concerto for Orchestra, Hovhaness's *Mysterious Mountain, Op. 132*, Roy Orbison, soundtracks of original Broadway muscials.

Rostov sighed. Too much. There was too much to pinpoint the man. Too much was the same as nothing.

"Mikal," Nikko called.

Rostov walked over to where Nikko knelt and stooped down beside him.

Nikko dabbed his fingers in the moist red blood on the floor. The puddle was barely the size of a half-dollar. "He was hit."

Rostov shook his head. "He's been hit before. The body, Nikko. Only the body will do."

Pietro Stollo stood on what was left of the dock and watched Rostov and the others comb through the trash for some sign of the American. He tapped his fingers impatiently on the stock of his H&K MP-5 SMG. He hated standing here, guarding this stupid boat with the big fan on its back. This was not a job for a member of the Red Brigade. After all, he had kidnapped three judges in Rome, executed two of them himself. Why not let the Iraqi guard the boat, or one of the PLO Arabs?

He stepped backward, his foot brushing something. He turned around, saw the black watch sitting on the dock, dripping wet. Why hadn't they noticed it before? He stared at it a moment, then looked around to see if the others saw it. It could have just been blown here by one of the explosions, overlooked as Rostov and the others rushed for the house. It looked expensive.

Pietro Stollo bent over to pick up the watch, not sure whether to tell the others or just keep it for himself. It was much better than his own.

As his fingers grazed the watch, a hand shot out of the water, reached up, grabbed him around the mouth, and yanked him under with hardly a splash.

He tried to breathe, arms and legs thrashing uselessly underwater as two powerful hands choked his throat. He tugged at the hands, digging at the fingers, but they were immovable. He opened his mouth to scream. Nothing. One tiny air bubble floated from his mouth toward the surface. He thought of the surface, less than a foot above. He could see the sun through the watery haze, see the air he so desperately needed. His lungs burned, his heart thumped.

Then nothing.

Hunter stuffed Pietro's dead body under what was left of the dock and began fishing for the H&K MP-5 SMG. He could see Rostov and the others picking through the charred remains that had been Hunter's life for the past couple of years. It was his own fault, he reasoned. He'd been warned that Rostov was around. He just hadn't expected him to jeopardize whatever mission he was on for some lousy revenge. Nikko had always been able to reason with Rostov, control those insane impulses, keep his mind on business. If Nikko couldn't do that anymore, the world was in for some bad times.

Hunter's hands swept through the water, dug into the mud and silt, looking for the gun. It had to be here somewhere.

That's when Rostov saw him.

"There!" Rostov screamed, pointing. "Kill him!"

Rostov, Nikko, Koyo, and the other terrorist all swung around in unison, bringing their weapons up. Rostov didn't have time to load another grenade into his M-203 launcher, so he shouldered the attached M-16 and began firing on automatic.

A spray of bullets plopped into the water around him. No longer concerned about silence, Hunter grabbed the rim of the airboat and pulled himself up and inside. A burst of gunfire chewed the hull near his head. Hunter quickly leaped to the controls, started the motor, muscled the boat into a 180-degree turn, and sped away, squinting into the wind, his hair flying wildly. He looked back over his shoulder, saw Rostov waving the other boats to come back and pick them up. The terrorists had stopped shooting while waiting for the boats to dock.

Hunter felt a little twitch at his mouth. Okay, a grin. It was crazy, but, hell, so was catching alligators.

He banked the airboat in another 180-degree U-turn and headed straight for his own dock. And Rostov.

There wasn't much time for them to react. The other boats immediately swerved away, bumping each other in their frenzy. A few terrorists dove into the swamp. Koyo and Nikko wisely threw themselves on their stomachs. Rostov and one other young fanatic stood their ground, aiming their weapons and firing at the approaching airboat.

But Hunter was coming too fast. He used the sunken part of the dock for a ramp and drove straight up it. The boat was catapulted into the air over the terrorists' heads. Except one. The young terrorist standing next to Rostov, teeth gritted, face contorted with bloodlust. The hull of the boat clipped his head, cracking the skull open from forehead to nose like a soft-boiled egg, spilling its mushy contents over the deck.

Hunter's boat continued on through his house. In a blur he saw the jumbled goods, the personal items, the books and cassettes. There on the floor, a photograph of John

Eagle and Hunter standing next to their biggest alligator, twenty-eight feet, their arms around each other, the Indian pouring a warm beer over Hunter's head. Maybe he imagined seeing it. He felt as if he were passing through someone else's life. Then he was gone, bouncing down on the water again and speeding off toward the Pay-hay-okee Overlook. A quick glance over his shoulder showed him what he already knew: Rostov and the others were jumping into their boats and coming after him.

Hunter gunned the motor and the boat lurched ahead at top speed.

The others followed.

Rostov and Tomas were in the first boat, along with two of their comrades. Nikko, Kurt, Koyo, and two others were in the second boat. The third boat held four armed terrorists.

Geysers of water shot up around Hunter's boat as the grenades and LAW missiles exploded around him. Water and mud speckled Hunter as he navigated his boat in a zigzag pattern, skimming the surface like a water spider. One explosion off the bow nearly flipped the airboat, but Hunter wrestled it back under control. But that allowed Rostov's gang to gain a few more precious feet on him.

A volley of bullets chewed up a section of hull less than a yard from Hunter's foot. He swerved the boat, and the next chatter of gunfire spit bullets into the water where he'd just been.

The wind whipped stinging water into his face and he squinted, studying the terrain ahead. He knew it pretty well by now, though not as well as John Eagle. Maybe he should head over toward Mahogany Hammock, try to lose them in the thickets. Or zip across the Whitewater Bay, find some help on Cape Sable. He shook his head. No use.

He couldn't keep outrunning them. It was just a matter of time before they caught up or blew him out of the water, or he ran out of gas. In the meantime, he pushed the airboat as hard as it would go.

Rostov launched another grenade. His shoulder was slightly sore from the repeated recoil, but he hardly noticed it as he watched the grenade arc through the air and plop into the water four feet from Hunter's snaking boat. The grenade detonated, merely spitting a wave of muddy water over Hunter.

"Damn," Rostov said. He spun back to face Tomas, who was piloting the boat. "Faster!"

"This is as fast as it goes," Tomas shouted over the roar of the engine.

"Then at least keep up with him. He's going around the bend there. We're losing sight of him."

"We can't do any better. We're too heavy."

"Too heavy," Rostov repeated. Gripping the edge of the boat, he walked unsteadily, fighting the sharp wind. When he was within reach, he lashed out with his foot and booted the third terrorist in the spine. The man's hands flew up from the impact and he somersaulted over the side and into the water. The boat immediately picked up speed. Rostov glared at Tomas. "So much for too heavy. Now catch up or I'll make this boat even lighter."

Tomas angled the boat around the bend.

"Shit!" Rostov yelled, kicking the side of the boat.

Before them lay an intersection of six different channels leading in six different directions. Hunter was nowhere to be seen.

Rostov made a slicing gesture across his throat and

Tomas immediately stopped the boat and waited for the others to catch up.

"Give it up, Mikal," Nikko urged. "We have wasted enough time on this Matt Hunter. He means nothing."

"Nikko, you take your boat down there." Rostov pointed. "You others follow that one. Tomas and I will search this channel."

"And what if he is not in any of these three channels?" Nikko asked.

"Then we meet back here and search the other three. And if we still do not find him, we search all six again. Is that clear, Nikko?"

Nikko looked into Rostov's wild eyes and nodded. It was useless to reason with him now, while he was in the grip of his obsession. "Yes, Mikal."

The three boats sped off in different directions.

In the third boat, Reneta Knoll was highest ranking of the four terrorists. She'd been recruited directly from the scattered remnants of the Baader-Meinhof Gang, living in a garage in Munich with her lovers, Gretchen and Wilhelm. Then one day Gretchen and Wilhelm, bourgeois pigs that she always knew they were, ran off and married each other, leaving Reneta a short note about their love for her and love for The Cause. She had spit on the note and flushed it down the toilet. They had grown weak waiting, had returned to their old values. Not Reneta. She had set bombs in Jewish restaurants in Frankfurt, shot the legs off an American diplomat in Bonn. She still believed, was willing to do what had to be done.

"Slowly," she hissed at the pilot. The channel was narrow, bordered on both sides by tall trees she couldn't name, with clumps of stringy gray Spanish moss hanging from the branches. She flipped her Uzi, yanked out the old clip, and snapped in a fresh thirty-two-round magazine.

"I see something," said the Cuban whose name she couldn't remember. "There, under the tree."

She gestured to the pilot and he slowed the boat even more. Reneta shaded her eyes with her hand and peered across the channel. She could barely see it, but, yes, there was the tip of a boat hidden under the low branches of that tree. She snapped her fingers at the pilot and pointed. He nodded, eased the boat to the opposite shore, directly across from the hidden boat. The four of them lined up, aimed their weapons at Hunter's boat, and at Reneta's command, opened fire.

Across the channel, the boat exploded into hundreds of fragments as the bullets ripped and shredded it. When a clip was empty, another was inserted and the firing continued.

The metallic clattering was so loud that they didn't notice the rustling in the tree above them. Didn't notice Matt Hunter leaping from an overhanging branch.

Hunter dropped straight down on the back of the Cuban, one knee slamming into the man's spine, the other knee impacting right behind his neck. The Cuban sprawled forward, his neck broken, dead before he'd ever known what caused the explosion of light and needles in his brain.

Hunter grabbed his SMG, dodging to the side just as one of the other terrorists spun and fired at him. The bullets whizzed by Hunter's ear, ripping a gaping hole in the fan housing at the back of the boat. Hunter returned fire, stitching a neat row of red buttons up the terrorist's neck.

The woman and the other man turned toward him simultaneously. No time to shoot both. He leaped with all his weight on the edge of the boat, tipping it just enough to knock the two terrorists off balance. She fired an automatic burst into trees. The man's barrage ate up another section of fan housing as the bullets pinged into the idle blades.

A sudden explosion in the water off the stern reminded Hunter of the other terrorists. He glanced back and saw Rostov's and Nikko's boats churning toward him. Hunter was also off balance, but he used the opportunity to dive for the boat's controls, opening the throttle as far as it would go. The boat lurched ahead, knocking the woman to the floor. Her gun skidded across the bottom of the boat. The man fought for balance, his arms windmilling. Hunter lifted his SMG and pointed it at the man, but the woman had recovered enough to throw a punch at his crotch. He turned just in time to take the blow on the thigh, but it still hurt. She was not weak. She reached out for her Uzi while her comrade regained enough equilibrium to point his Uzi at Hunter's chest.

Hunter snapped out a side kick to the man's forehead and, without lowering his leg, fired off two more kicks to the man's chin and throat. The terrorist grasped his own neck as he flew backwards off the boat.

Another grenade, this one from Kurt, exploded in the water next to the terrorist, pulverizing his head, sending a spray of red hunks up with the geyser of water.

Her hand around her Uzi, the woman was firing from her back now.

Hunter felt his SMG shatter from the impact of her bullets as the useless gun was ripped from his hands. Anticipating another burst of bullets, Hunter jumped off the speeding boat, but hung on to the side as it roared across the water, straight down the narrow channel. The water pulled at his clothes and limbs. A couple of times he felt his legs bump a submerged log in the shallow water.

The woman was up on one knee now, swinging her Uzi around toward Hunter's head. His SMG was somewhere in the water a hundred yards behind them by now. Unarmed, clinging to the speeding boat, with Rostov and his men gaining on him, an armed terrorist about to shoot him, thinking no other choice. He let go with one hand, plunged it into the water, his fingers shoveling along the silty bottom of the water. A sharp rock sliced through the side of his wrist. A larger rock smashed a knuckle. Yet he managed to scoop up a handful of mud and fling it directly into the woman's face just as she was about to squeeze the trigger. The mud splatted in her eyes, and her burst of gunfire was diverted a few inches over Hunter's head. The distraction gave him enough time to haul himself back into the boat, roll over once, and kick her in the stomach. The impact hurled her backwards into the fan housing, her right elbow snapping back through the gaping hole where the bullets had eaten away the protective wire.

The giant fan blades whacked indifferently at her elbow, shredding bone and flesh with terrible efficiency. Reneta screamed, stumbled forward, cradling her mangled arm to her chest as if uncertain it was still attached. She never found out. A burst of gunfire from Rostov's boat aimed at Hunter pounded into her back, kicking her off the boat.

Hunter crawled to the controls, and the boat swerved just ten yards before it nosed into an ancient tree trunk, thick as a temple pillar.

The two remaining boats raced after him.

From the east, behind a large hammock, Hunter heard another airboat, its engine revving at a high pitch. He couldn't see it yet, but knew it would soon round the hammock in front of him with a clear shot straight at him. With the two boats behind him and a third about to charge from the front, Hunter didn't see a lot of options. He jerked the boat toward the bank, letting the overhanging branches shield him from sight for a few seconds. Hunter slung the SMG over his shoulder. As his boat passed under a sturdy branch, he reached up and snagged it, hoisting himself up into the tree. Beneath him his airboat drifted on, bumping the shore as it continued downstream.

He climbed higher into the tree. The long spongy moss smelled like clothes that had been stored in a damp basement for too long. He eased his body out a little farther on the limb, anchoring himself where several branches formed a small cradle. He lifted the SMG and waited.

His airboat must have made its way out of the underbrush, because Rostov was pointing and waving for the other boat to follow his lead. Hunter recognized some of the men, though he hadn't met them before. Their photographs were familiar to anti-terrorist groups around the world, hanging in hundreds of offices just as Dillinger's photo had once been featured in police stations and banks. There was Nikko Kador, half-Russian, half-Hungarian, the only one who could keep Rostov's insanity in check. Apparently Hunter's last confrontation with Rostov had pushed him a little over the edge and his Soviet bosses had felt a stabilizing influence was necessary. Hunter recognized Koyo Gotoda instantly. He'd been a guiding force in the Japanese Red Army, one of the planners of the 1977 JAL hijacking in Bombay in exchange for six million dollars and the release of six Red Army prisoners. The Japanese government had given in and Koyo'd disappeared in Baghdad. Kurt Schnell, once with the Baader-Meinhof, then with anyone who could use a man of his talents, had once tortured an entire family after he'd already gotten the information he wanted. Tomas had no known last name. He was Colombian, a drug-runner whose sexual preference for boys and girls under the age of ten had gotten him in trouble with his own people. Still, his contacts with underground sources had made him valuable; he'd been recruited by Rostov, who not only tolerated Tomas's perverse sexuality, but often supplied him with the objects of his desire.

Hunter sighed. Quite a little collection of humanity. He shouldered the SMG, waiting for Rostov's boat. He wiped the sweat out of his eyes and aimed down the barrel. Just a little bit closer, he thought, recalling the title of a song by Jay and the Americans. He and Mary Kay Diehl had often made out to it. He frowned at the memory. Times had changed.

As Rostov's two boats came toward him, he finally saw the rustling of saw grass and brush where the third mystery boat was. Rostov heard it too, for he swung around just as the airboat burst out of the brush, slicing between the two terrorists' boats.

"Holy shit," Hunter muttered. "John Eagle."

John Eagle was steering the boat with one hand and aiming his old double-barreled shotgun with the other. He squeezed off two rounds at Rostov as he roared by. Both missed the Russian, but the second round caught one of the other terrorists in the face, the buckshot wiping away everything to the right of his nose. Tomas wasted no time in tossing the dead man overboard while Rostov quickly fired a grenade from his launcher. The grenade flew past John Eagle and exploded harmlessly on the far bank of the hammock.

John Eagle's attack had disrupted Rostov's approach.

Hunter tried to shift his position to get off a shot, but they were still too far away. "Get out of there, John Eagle," Hunter said quietly. "Get the hell out. This isn't your fight."

Almost as if he'd heard, John Eagle swerved his boat to the right and disappeared into a thicket of tall grass.

"After him!" Rostov roared.

Both boats turned toward the thicket. Hunter could see them through the dripping moss in front of him, but he couldn't get a clear shot.

Just as the two boats were about to plow into the thicket, John Eagle's boat shot out from behind them. His shotgun was loaded again, and he pointed it with one hand at Nikko and Kurt's boat. Everyone dove for cover just as John Eagle pulled the trigger. His shots missed the men, but chipped off a couple of bite-sized chunks from the edge of the boat. Instantly, his boat slipped back into the tall grass.

Rostov went after John Eagle, gesturing for Nikko to come in at the opposite angle so they could catch the Indian between them as if in a nutcracker.

Hunter watched their maneuver down the barrel of his SMG, patiently awaiting a shot. This way, John Eagle, he thought. Bring them this way.

Rostov's boat waited quietly in the water while Nikko tried to chase John Eagle toward it. Suddenly John Eagle buzzed out of the grass again, barely missing Rostov's boat. John Eagle lifted his reloaded shotgun again and fired. A fistful of buckshot clanged into the spinning fan. Rostov, Tomas, and the other terrorists hugged the bottom of the boat.

Then the grass parted and Nikko's boat exploded out of the grass thicket and rammed into John Eagle's hull, almost knocking the old Seminole off his feet. But he recovered quickly and lifted his shotgun at Rostov, who was loading another grenade into his launcher. Behind him, Nikko was aiming his gun at John Eagle's back.

Hunter stood on the branch and shouted a warning. "Get out of there, John! Go!"

John Eagle turned and gazed up at the tree where Hunter was perched. He smiled at Hunter. "I'll get you, man. Hang on." He started to turn the boat around.

Nikko fired. Five 9mm parabellum bullets climbed the ladder of John Eagle's spine, shattering each vertabra they touched. John Eagle flopped face down, dead.

Hunter squeezed the trigger of his SMG, raking Rostov's boat. Rostov dove out of the way, but one bullet drilled through Tomas's hand.

"He's up there," Rostov said, once more aiming his grenade launcher. He fired and the grenade hurtled toward Hunter's tree with deadly speed. When it hit, the tree exploded in a smoky swirl of wood chips and wet moss. Some burning branches dropped into the water with a sizzling hiss. Mud shot twenty feet into the air.

The two airboats waded slowly through the debris. Rostov leaned over the side, kicking at the floating tree branches and hunks of bark.

"He must be dead," Kurt said.

"Where's the body?" Rostov said.

They continued searching.

"Here!" Nikko said excitedly. "Look." He leaned over the side and fished an SMG rifle butt out of the water. It had been blown in half. "He was holding this."

Rostov nodded, pleased. "Now we must find the body."

"For pity's sake, Mikal," Nikko said. "We can waste no more time on this foolishness. We have appointments to keep this evening. We can wait no longer. This Hunter could not have survived. No man could.''

Rostov looked at his watch, rubbed the scar on his wrist. He stared a long hard minute at the water, examining each piece of debris. "Yes, we must go back now. He must be dead.''

The two boats moved away at top speed. Rostov looked back over his shoulder at the burning tree stump, the floating bits of wood. He frowned.

They were out of sight when the water began to ripple. Movement. A bubble floated to the surface, broke, sending concentric circles across the water. Then another bubble. Then dozens. Finally Hunter could no longer hold his breath, and his head bobbed above the water. A long bloody gash cleaved his chest where a spiked branch had gouged him, ripping his shirt and chest. He sucked in a lungful of precious air, then let it out slowly, like opium smoke. Again. And again. He fought the dizziness, ignored the ache behind his eyeballs. He didn't need to put his hand on the back of his scalp. He knew there was a lump there. He knew it was bleeding.

John Eagle's boat had drifted to shore across the inlet. His friend's arm hung over the side, the fingertips dangling in the water as if he were on a lazy picnic cruise. Hunter swam for the boat.

Hunter nudged the airboat up to the sunken dock. Gently he lifted John Eagle in his arms and carried him into what was left of his house. John Eagle had helped him build this house. So had Clark Little Hawk and Prince Charles.

One Sunday while working on the dock, the three men had gotten so drunk that they didn't notice two curious alligators who'd come to investigate. Prince Charles had chased them away by throwing Hunter's shoes at them. John Eagle had swum drunkenly after one of the 'gators, dragged it ashore, and wrestled it onto its back. Then he'd jammed Hunter's shoes onto its feet. "Think we got ya a girl friend, Hunter," he'd said, laughing so hard tears splashed down his cheeks. That was how Hunter would always remember him. Laughing.

Hunter lowered John Eagle's body onto the shattered bed. He reached over to a section of wall that was still standing and tore off a colorful Indian blanket. Carefully he draped it over his friend.

Hunter looked around the shambles of the place. He found some jeans and a shirt, quickly changing out of his mud-encrusted clothes. There was nothing else he wanted or needed. What he wanted and needed was miles away by now: Rostov.

He grabbed the overturned kerosene lantern from the floor, lit it, and walked away from the house with it. At the edge of the dock he paused. The Everglades was quiet like it sometimes got toward dusk, just as the day creatures retired and the night creatures emerged. Hunter climbed into his boat, started the motor, and gave his house and friend one final look. The house was nothing to him. A place where he had once lived, nothing more. He had lived many places in his life, always knew each was temporary. But his friend was something else. That was forever.

Hunter threw the kerosene lantern into the air, steering the airboat away before the lantern fell. Behind him he heard the shattered glass, heard the whoosh of fire spreading across the wood floor, smelled the bitter smoke of his past.

As he guided the boat across the saw grass he realized that no matter what happened now, he would never be able to come back here to live. As usual, his presence had brought harm to those close to him. Never again.

By the time he reached John Eagle's place it was completely dark. Hunter tied the airboat up and stepped onto the dock, which stuck out from the shore like a little dog's tail. Behind the dock was his friend's cabin. It was modest and homey, the same cabin in which John Eagle had been born, the same one in which he'd outlived two wives and raised three children, all three now living in big cities somewhere. Next to the cabin was John Eagle's prized truck, a four-wheel drive Dodge that he polished weekly, joking, "This is the reason God put the white man on earth. To build these babies."

Hunter slid behind the wheel, plucked the extra key from the ashtray, and started up the engine. In the rearview mirror he could see the glow of the fire consuming his house. He slammed the gear shift into first and spun the truck out of there. Four years ago he had taken himself out of the crazy game. Now he was dealing himself back in for one last hand of showdown.

6

Adams came into the restaurant through the back entrance. The rickety old screen door creaked as he stepped into the small kitchen. A heavy black woman in her fifties looked up at him. She wore an apron that said MAMA D'S CREOLE COOKIN'. Her face shone with sweat from the steaming kettles on the ancient gas stove. She looked Adams up and down, then turned her attention back to one of the steaming kettles. She dipped a ladle in, then lifted it out. The thick soupy contents boiled in the ladle. Without blowing on it or cooling it in any way, she took a sip.

"You ain't never had gumbo, till you had my gumbo, boy," she said, chuckling. "Make your face scrunch up with delight. Better than sex." She laughed loudly. "Sometimes."

"I'm looking for—"

"I know what you're lookin' for, boy." She nodded toward the batwing doors that led to the restaurant. "Hunter

73

don't never come to Miami without lookin' up his own Mama D. He's waitin' on you.''

Adams started toward the batwing doors, then paused. He couldn't let an opportunity like this pass. ''You known Hunter a long time?''

''Long time.'' She sprinkled some brown spice from an unmarked jar into one of the kettles. ''Long, long time.''

''He's mentioned you often. Said you reminded him of home, where he grew up. I wonder why.''

Mama D laughed, her massive breasts and stomach jiggling. ''Nice try. Don't you never give up tryin'.'' She laughed again and dumped some yellow powder into the kettle.

Adams pushed through the batwing doors, pausing to let his eyes adjust to the much darker dining area. The room was small, holding just six tables. All six were occupied, and outside the front door Adams could see half a dozen people lined up waiting for one to become available.

In the rear, his back to the wall, sat Hunter. Gunfighter's seat, Adams thought wryly.

He walked over to Hunter's table and sat down. Hunter was spooning gumbo into his mouth.

''How is it?'' Adams asked.

''Terrible. Mama D makes the worst gumbo in the South.''

''She does a good business.''

''She's made a lot of friends. They eat here anyway.''

Adams looked at Hunter. ''You putting me on, Matt?''

Hunter pushed his bowl across the table. ''Try it.''

Adams tasted the gumbo. He made a sour face. ''It's terrible.''

''That's what I said. Mama D used to be Professor Dietrich. Taught Quantum Physics for years at Yale. Worked some sensitive government projects too. She also speaks five languages fluently. Thing is, she always wanted to open a restaurant. Took early retirement a few years ago, and here she is.''

"How'd you come to know her? Yale?"

Hunter pulled his bowl of gumbo back and finished the last few spoonfuls. When he looked up at Adams, he said, "I'll take the assignment."

"Great, Matt, I'll—"

Hunter stood, picked up the check, stuffed it in Adams's breast pocket. "I usually leave a twenty-percent tip."

"Wait, Matt, we have to talk. Details—"

But Hunter was already walking toward the door.

7

Rostov looked at his watch. The luminous dial gave an eerie green glow to the hands and numbers. 1:25 a.m. Peeking out from under his watch were the pale rubbery tips of the scar. The H Hunter had carved there. Rostov rubbed his wrist.

"You can have that removed, you know," Nikko said, standing next to him on the beach. "I've read that doctors can remove scars. Skin grafts, laser surgery, all kinds of things."

Rostov stared out across the dark sea, breathed the tangy salt air deep into his lungs. "Yes, perhaps one day. When I am certain."

"He is dead, Mikal. You saw the tree, what was left of his gun."

"And I know the man, Nikko."

Nikko sighed. "Do you see them yet?"

Rostov raised the Startron Mark 424 Series 4 night scope to his eyes. What little moonlight leaked through the thick cloud covering was enough for him to pick up the shimmery outlines of the assault crafts heading toward them. "They are coming. All six of them."

"Excellent!" Nikko said, rubbing his hands together.

Tim had one finger under her bra and was going for a second.

"Wait," she said, and he was afraid she was going to tell him to stop. But all she did was unhook the front of her bra and let her small round breasts fall free. "There, that's easier, isn't it?"

"Yeah, sure," Tim said. He hesitated. This was too good to be true. This was his first time parking with Belinda. They were in Library Science together but that didn't really count since she was editor of the school newspaper and was always getting excused from class to go on some assignment somewhere. She got A's anyway.

"Don't stop," Belinda said, guiding his hand back to her breast, arranging his fingers on her nipple. "That feels good." She reached over and gently squeezed his crotch through his jeans. "Just like that does."

Tim leaned over and kissed her, his eyes closed, his tongue halfway down her throat. If she swallowed, she'd probably yank his tonsils right out of his mouth, he thought. She pressed her breast into his hand and he flicked his thumb over the nipple. Her hand tensed around his crotch and he realized she was fumbling for his zipper. Jesus, what had he done to be so lucky? When he'd asked her out he hadn't even been sure his dad would lend him the car. She didn't care; she could always borrow her brother's. Which was what they were sitting in right now, her brother's brand-new red Fiero.

His hand drifted from her breast and slid up under her

skirt, fingers skating along the warm, soft inner thigh. She moaned, and the vibrations traveled along his tongue, up through his sinuses, and into his eyes. He could swear his eyeballs were vibrating. His index finger touched the edge of her panties. He felt bristly hairs there. She squeezed his crotch again in encouragement.

He had three fingers under her panties when he heard the noise. A tapping at the window, like a small bird pecking. At first he ignored it, thinking it might just be his imagination. After all, his senses were going a little crazy right now. Besides, they were at the remotest damn beach on the coast. Few people came here during the day, let alone the middle of the night.

But there it was again. Tap, tap, tap.

Tim opened his eyes and looked into Belinda's eyes. She opened them slowly and dreamily. Then suddenly they were wide and she was pushing at him, screaming.

Tim twisted around, smacking his elbow on the gear shift and cracking his knee on the steering wheel. But he hardly noticed the pain. He was too afraid to feel anything.

Encircling the new red Fiero were at least fifty men clad entirely in black, each carrying a deadly looking rifle like something out of a James Bond movie. And there, tapping on the windshield was a tall handsome blond man, smiling at them. The tall man made a gesture for Tim to roll down the window.

"Don't do it, Tim!" Belinda shouted.

"Why not? They're probably marines or something."

"What are marines doing out here?"

"I don't know." Tim shrugged. "Maneuvers. War games, maybe."

"Start the car."

Tim looked at the blond man who was still smiling.

More armed men were drifting up from the beach. Tim reached for the key and turned it. The motor rumbled to life.

The blond man frowned sadly, lifted a pistol to the windshield, and aimed at Tim's face.

"Jesus!" Tim cried, frantically throwing the gear shift into first just as Rostov's bullet punched through the windshield and drilled through his forehead and brain. Belinda's scream was cut short by Rostov's second shot, the bullet entering just above the left ear and exiting below the right.

Rostov looked up at Nikko. "You said this beach is always deserted."

"Yes, that's what the report said."

"Continue with the landing."

Nikko led the black-clad terrorists along the dune where they could watch the remaining three landing crafts pull close to shore. They scraped along the sand, dropped their gates like bread boxes opening, and fifty more terrorists from each craft scampered down the ramp, through the shallow water, and up the beach to join the others. In all, three hundred men and women, each trained in the deadliest, most ruthless forms of domestic terrorism, surrounded Nikko and Rostov on the deserted Florida beach.

When they had all amassed and stood silently waiting, Rostov bestowed a smile on them. "This way," he said. They followed silently, the three hundred pairs of marching feet sounding like nothing more than the fluttering wings of a flock of sea gulls.

As they climbed over the last dune, they could see the line of vehicles parked along the access road. Dozens of vans, station wagons, trucks, and cars of every description awaited them.

"Commanders, front and center," Rostov snapped, and

a line of men formed in front of him. He pointed to the first VW van and said, "Seattle."

The commander nodded and waved to the crowd. Six terrorists peeled away from the others and followed him to the van. They climbed in and drove away.

"Chicago," Rostov told the next man, and continued to assign transportation and destinations until there were no more troops or vehicles left.

Nikko stood next to Rostov, watching the line of headlights as the terrorists convoyed to the highway. "In eighteen hours, the United States will be a very different place."

"It has been coming."

"The Americans have grown soft, a nation of weeping children. We will give them something to weep about."

Rostov laughed. "We are not politicos, Nikko. Let us not stoop to rhetoric. We are soldiers, trained to kill. Let us confine our speeches to that subject."

"Then let the killing begin," Nikko said.

Rostov smiled. "It already has."

8

Dahlia McGuire tapped Lt. Green on the shoulder. When he turned around, she snapped his photo with her camera. "Gotcha, Lieutenant."

"McGuire." His voice was weary, frustrated.

"What's going on?" She gestured at the army of uniformed cops sifting through the sand at various intervals, the team of fingerprint specialists dusting the red Fiero.

"How'd you get here, McGuire?"

"My jeep, Lieutenant."

"Don't start, Dahlia."

"Okay, okay. I got a phone tip."

"Anonymous, right?"

"My favorite kind. Told me there was an 'interesting development' in that Coast Guard case. Told me to come right out here."

Lt. Green scratched his head, patted his thinning hair in place. "Describe the voice."

"I don't know. A man's. Deep. Maybe foreign, or

maybe he just had a cold. Hard to tell. Kind of nasal, you know?''

"Yeah. Some guy who called Timboldt at the *Globe* and De Vries from Channel Seven."

"What?" she bristled. "The bastard called those guys too?"

"And he must have called them first, 'cause they've already come and gone. I shooed them away myself."

"Damn! Jerk calls me at five in the goddamn morning, tells me to hotfoot it out here for an exclusive. Some damn exclusive. What happened here anyway?"

"Nothing special. A couple of kids got murdered."

She studied his chubby face, the sunken gray eyes. "You got at least fifty guys out there playing patty-cake in the sand. You want me to believe that's the kind of manpower you use for nothing special?"

"Maybe I lost my cigarette case."

"You don't smoke."

"How can I when I lost my cigarette case?"

McGuire smiled. "Okay, Lieutenant. But you know if the guy called once, he'll call again. Obviously some kind of publicity nut."

"Everybody wants to be famous sometimes. Even me. I'd have knocked 'em dead on the old *Ed Sullivan Show*. I do pretty good impressions."

"Yeah. Let me see the one of the kindly police lieutenant helping the reporter get a scoop."

Lt. Green laughed. "You never quit, McGuire."

"Neither do you, Lieutenant. I know a snow job, even in Miami. This casual bantering means you're trying to keep me away from something. What?"

Lt. Green's smile shifted into a frown. He leaned forward and lowered his voice. "Go home, Dahlia. There are things going on around here they won't even tell me about. You get in their way and they'll run right over you."

"You talking about whoever did this or the people investigating it?"

Lt. Green's frown deepened. "Yes."

She felt a little shaken. Lt. Green was the toughest, fairest man she'd ever known, a man who'd managed to stay decent and compassionate despite his long years on the force. Yet he still had the respect and fear of some of Miami's hardest criminals. He was not a man who scared easily. But Dahlia knew he was scared now. She watched his eyes drift over her shoulders to Harmon and Leeds, the two local FBI agents, and the man from the CIA, Adams.

"Gotta go," Lt. Green said. "Can I trust you to leave?"

She nodded. "Okay, Bill."

He smiled at her and walked off to join the other three men. The two FBI agents were pointing to a series of tire tracks in front of them. They all four kneeled down to examine them.

McGuire walked slowly toward her jeep, screwing the telephoto lens onto her camera. She would keep her word to Lt. Green, but in the meantime she was taking in as much of the scene as possible, occasionally pausing to snap a photograph of the cops at work, the Fiero, the federal agents. Through her viewfinder she saw Adams suddenly jerk around, as if he felt a presence. Her eye pressed to the viewfinder, she followed Adams's line of vision with her camera, back, back, back to a tall dune near the edge of the road. Standing there next to a big shiny pickup truck was a handsomely rugged man in a straw cowboy hat. He was surveying the scene with a cool gaze, squinting against the early morning sun.

McGuire swung the camera back to Adams. She expected to see him sending a couple of cops up to question the man, the usual procedure for dealing with people who got past the police lines. But Adams didn't make a move. He merely looked at the stranger for a minute and then— this was odd—he seemed to relax a little, turning back to the others as if relieved by the man's presence.

McGuire turned her camera on the stranger, only now he had a pair of binoculars and was staring at her. She pressed the shutter button and snapped his picture. It was more a defense reflex than a conscious movement. He lowered his binoculars and she thought she saw a tiny smile on his lips. Then she noticed that under his arm he had a copy of the *Herald*. She couldn't tell if it was turned to the page with her story and by-line, but somehow she sensed it was. That the stranger knew not only Adams, but her as well.

She swung the camera back to Adams, but he was busily discussing something with Lt. Green. When she turned her camera to the stranger agan, he was gone. So was his truck.

9

Benjamin Shapiro was nervous. His skin was clammy and his stomach rumbled so loudly that he was certain the rabbi would notice. He felt like a prisoner planning an escape right under the warden's nose.

The rest of the congregation, his parents included, were busily singing a blessing or prayer that Benjamin did not totally understand. He didn't understand most of what went on in the synagogue, even though he was to be bar mitzvahed the following week, right in the middle of Chanukah. The bar mitzvah was not his idea; his parents had insisted, despite Benjamin's patient explanation that he did not believe in Judaism or any other religion for that matter. His father said that once he was thirteen and bar mitzvahed he could believe or not believe in any goddamn thing he wanted. "But until then," he'd concluded sternly, "study your Hebrew and do what the rabbi tells you."

Now, as a special honor, Benjamin was to light the first candle for Chanukah in front of the whole congregation.

His Hebrew was passable, good enough to get him through the blessings without a mistake. It was the singing that worried him. His voice was just beginning to do funny things, cracking sometimes and suddenly shooting up three octaves as if someone had stomped on his foot. It was embarrassing.

The congregation was finishing the prayer, having a little trouble staying together because the cantor had introduced a new tune with the words. The words were thousands of years old; the tune was two days old.

"Benjamin," Rabbi Kramer whispered.

Benjamin stood up, his legs wobbly as he marched to the center of the altar where giant menorah, donated by Fein's Fine Furnishings, stood. The rabbi held a box of Diamond wooden matches. He nodded.

Benjamin sang, "*Beruch atoh adonoy . . .*" So far his voice was holding up fine. The rabbi was lighting the servant candle in the middle of the menorah. He handed it to Benjamin so he could light the first candle. Benjamin continued singing as he touched the small flame to the wick: ". . . *lazzman hazzah.*"

Benjamin's concentration was so great that he didn't notice the shouting at first. Then he heard the doors at the back being slammed opened, heard the footsteps and the angry shouts. He turned, a drop of hot wax dripping onto his hand.

But he didn't flinch. He was too shocked by what he saw.

A dozen men were stampeding through the congregation. They all wore brown uniforms and red armbands with black swastikas. Nazis in the synagogue! There were horrified screams from some, outraged hollering from others. But the Nazis didn't pay any attention. Some carried guns, some baseball bats—Louisville sluggers like Benjamin had at home—some cans of spray paint.

Old Mr. Horowitz, whom everyone knew had survived Dachau forty years ago, sat in his chair and watched with great sadness. Benjamin could almost see the man deflate, compress to a place inside himself where nothing could touch him. But his son, David, leaped to his feet and grabbed one of the Nazis by the collar and punched him in the nose. Another Nazi rushed over and clubbed David Horowitz on the head so hard that everyone gasped. David dropped to the floor unconscious or dead, Benjamin couldn't tell which.

A couple of Nazis climbed up to the ark, knocked the rabbi and cantor aside, pulled open the velvet curtain, and set fire to the torah. Two other Nazis began spray-painting giant red swastikas on the walls.

The congregation watched, some with fear, others with hate.

"Go back to Africa with your nigger friends, you Jew pigs," one Nazi said.

That was too much for Mr. Kleinman, the Phys. Ed. teacher at Benjamin's high school. He lunged at the Nazi doing the talking, but before he could reach him, the Nazi pulled out a pistol and fired two shots into Mr. Kleinman's chest.

"One less Jew to stink up our country," the man who shot him said.

No one moved or said anything.

The Nazi smiled and started walking toward the doors, slowly, as if daring anyone to try anything. The other Nazis followed him. When they were all gathered at the back of the room, the head Nazi grabbed a rifle from one of the others and fired a burst into the congregation. There were screams as everyone dove for the ground. Everyone except old Mr. Horowitz, who remained sitting in his chair, his back to the Nazis.

Benjamin hugged the carpeted altar as the Nazi fired another burst into the crowd. Then all the Nazis were gone. The sound of their heavy boots running down the hallway echoed in Benjamin's mind long after they'd gone.

Outside the synagogue, Rostov and his terrorists climbed into their vans, the license plates of which could be traced to known members of radical white-supremacy groups. As they drove away, he removed his armband and stared at it. "Now these guys knew how to have a good time," he said.

At the same time, a few blocks from Meridian Avenue, the South Miami Community Center was having a Christmas dance. Most of the kids attending it were Cuban refugees or of Cuban descent. So far there'd only been three minor disturbances. One kid had got drunk and fallen, sitting down on the bottle of Southern Comfort he'd sneaked into the dance. Eighteen stitches on his right buttock. One boy had been thrown out for starting a fight after his girl friend danced with someone else. The girl friend stayed. And a girl of fifteen was sent home when she was caught in the men's lavatory performing sex acts for cash. Mr. Moncado, director of the center, wasn't upset. He'd had more trouble than this chaperoning dances at the rich high schools on Long Island.

The live band was called Taino, after the main tribe of people in Cuba when the Spanish first discovered it. They played a mixture of Latin, reggae, and Top 100 tunes. They weren't very good, but they'd fit the center's meager budget.

Tonio Santiago, trim and athletic, returned from the dance floor dripping with sweat. His friend Carlos Diego, also eighteen but chubby and shy, leaned against the wall sipping a Coke.

"Looking good, man," Carlos said.

"That Maria can really dance. You see the way she shakes her ass?"

Carlos blushed, looked into his Coke.

Tonio realized what was bothering his friend. "You wanna meet her, man?"

"No. You're the one dancing with her."

"Two dances. No big deal. Come on, I'll introduce you. She and her friends went outside to get some air."

Carlos didn't move.

"Come on," Tonio encouraged. "Don't be a chicken. She's real nice. You two will get along great."

Tonio dragged Carlos outside.

Maria and three other girls were standing in the parking lot. Maria was leaning against her brother's 1964 green Plymouth. Two of her friends were smoking cigarettes.

"I can't, man," Carlos said, stopping.

"Hey, just follow my lead. Do what I do. It's easy."

Carlos reluctantly tagged behind Tonio as they approached the girls. They could hear whispering and giggling as they got closer.

"Hey, Maria." Tonio waved. "Ladies."

"Tonio, Tonio, wherefore art thou, Tonio?" Carlotta said. More giggling.

"You're weird," Tonio said good-naturedly, and Carlotta smiled at the attention. After all, Tonio was a major hunk. "You all know Carlos."

A couple nodded, one shrugged. Maria said, "Hi, Carlos. How's Nina?"

Carlos's sister sometimes walked home from school with Maria. "Fine."

Suddenly they were all flooded in bright headlights. They shaded their eyes and turned to face the source of disturbance.

A squad car rolled into the parking lot.

The doors opened and two men in uniforms got out slowly.

"Oh, man," Tonio complained.

"What do they want?" Maria asked.

"Who knows? It's the same old bullshit with cops."

The two men ambled toward the kids, each carrying a shotgun.

Tonio shook his head. "They probably just want to frisk us like usual. Cop a cheap feel from you girls."

"This stinks," Carlotta said.

"Just pretend it was me." Tonio grinned.

"You wish."

The two men were only ten feet away now.

Tonio started to walk toward them. "Hey, man, can you give us a break this time? We got a dance going on."

The shorter man, the one wearing mirrored sunglasses despite the dark night, whipped his shotgun up and fired into Tonio's stomach. The impact sent Tonio flying backwards up onto the hood of the Plymouth, shattering the windshield.

Carlotta screamed.

Carlos grabbed Maria and threw her to the ground just as the two men opened fire. Carlotta caught a round in her head; her face disappeared in a pink mist. One of the other girls put her hands out to protect herself, but the shotgun pellets blew the hands away.

Mr. Moncado led the way out of the gymnasium/dance

floor, followed by dozens of kids. The two men opened fire on them, pumping round after round into the crowd, the shotguns smoking like factory chimneys.

"Let's go," the man in sunglasses said.

The other one aimed his shotgun at Carlos and Maria.

"No," the man in sunglasses said. "He wants witnesses."

The two of them hurried to the squad car, climbed in, and sped away, tires squealing. Inside the car, Koyo removed his sunglasses and nodded at Kurt. He turned in his seat and looked back at the parking lot. Some were crying as they tended the wounded and dead. Some ran frantically through the streets. Others remained hugging the ground, paralyzed with fear.

"Almost too easy," Koyo said, satisfied.

10

Dahlia McGuire licked the suction cup, grimaced at the rubbery taste, then slapped the cup onto the back of the phone receiver.

"You still fooling with that thing, McGuire?" Carl Peoples asked. He was one of the *Herald*'s top reporters, but a real pain in the ass to Dahlia. When he wasn't leering at her, he was trying to steal her stories.

"It's a new one," she said. "The other one wore out."

"We could test it out. I could call you, talk dirty." He grinned and winked.

"Thanks, but I wouldn't want to tax your vocabulary."

"You're such a bitch, McGuire. That's why I never call you."

"Then it's worth it, I guess."

"Yeah, well fuck you."

"Gee, I wish I'd said that."

Carl Peoples stormed off.

The phone rang. Dahlia pressed the Record and Play

buttons, took a deep breath, and plucked up the phone. "McGuire."

"McGuire, turn that damn thing off and get your skinny ass in here."

Dahlia twisted around in her chair and saw Metro editor Dan Logan grinning at her through the glass partition of his office. She hung up the phone and went in to see him.

"Hi, Chief," she said, sitting across from his cluttered desk.

"Don't call me Chief." It was a ritual they went through, straight from the Superman comics. But they'd been working together for five years now and had a good professional relationship. They respected each other. Sometimes Dan and his wife, June, had Dahlia over for dinner. Some at the paper thought Dahlia and Dan were having an affair because they were about the same age and the two best-looking people on the paper. They weren't. Dan was devoted to his wife and two daughters; Dahlia was devoted to her job. Still, for the benefit of the paper's gossip grapevine, they occasionally flirted in public.

"How's June's foot?" Dahlia asked.

"Still broken. She's going nuts trying to take a bath without getting it wet. Nearly drowned herself last night."

Dahlia nodded. She could tell by the thick blue vein on the side of Dan's neck that he was upset. "What's up?"

"What do you mean?" He gave her an innocent look, then remembered who he was talking to. His face sagged. "It's getting worse out there. I just got off the phone with Henson at the cop shop. Two officers were pelted with garbage over near Lummus Park. The whole Hispanic community is fired up, near rioting. Not just them. A bunch of Jewish Defense League toughs firebombed a

Nazi meeting place. At least we think it's JDL. They deny it, say it was someone pretending to be them.''

''What about the cops that started this?''

''Still haven't been identified. Cops say it wasn't any of theirs.''

''Try convincing the people of that.''

Dan shook his head. ''Yeah, well it's still news. And we gotta cover it. I'm just a little worried about June and the kids.''

''Send them away,'' Dahlia suggested.

''Where? You see the wire this morning? They've got trouble in Los Angeles. Chicanos and blacks are shooting each other over some rape and murder. In Detroit a Ford factory was bombed. Some union people claimed credit. Now the plant's closed, and all those people are out of work and angry. There've been threats. Michigan state police are guarding the plant now.''

''One thing's for damn sure, it can't be coincidence. It's got to have something to do with that Coast Guard cutter. The CIA and FBI are still sniffing around. They know something.''

''So what? The people rioting don't know that. Tell it to the friends of those dead kids at that community center. They just know that two guys in cops' uniforms blasted holes in their loved ones. They want vengeance.'' He rubbed his temples, sighed heavily. ''Vengeance, McGuire. Everybody in this country thinks they got a gripe against somebody else. You tap that anger and the released pressure would be enough to blow this country apart.''

''You don't think it's that bad?'' she asked.

He didn't answer. Instead he slid a tearsheet from the teletype machine.

Dahlia read it, then looked up. For the first time since

the chaos had begun, she felt truly scared. "Fifteen bombings across the country. Jesus."

"Mostly banks, social security offices where checks are processed, that sort of thing. There have been runs on banks in twelve states. Social security checks will be delayed by at least two weeks. Those people needing the money won't have anything. Two banks have already been closed down. Threaten people's money and the whole economic system folds up. Whoever's doing this knows just where to hit."

Dahlia heard her phone ring and jumped out of her chair. She saw Carl Peoples get up from his desk and head for hers. "Get away, Peoples," she screamed, racing between desks. She bumped him out of the way and grabbed the receiver.

"Just trying to help." Peoples shrugged.

"Hello, hello," she said breathlessly into the phone. "McGuire here."

"Relax, Ms. McGuire," the voice, the faintly foreign one, said. "Catch your breath. And don't forget to turn on your tape recorder."

"Thanks," she said, punching the buttons. "Haven't heard from you in a few days."

"I've been busy, or haven't you heard?"

"What do you mean by that? Heard what?"

The voice chuckled huskily. "Nice try, Ms. McGuire."

"Listen, pal, you called me. You got something to say, say it. I'm pretty busy here. I've got five more minutes left on my coffee break and this crossword puzzle's a bitch. What's a six-letter word for 'more than enough'?"

The phone was silent. Dahlia nodded at Dan Logan as he walked toward her. She felt her throat drying up, her tongue flopping helplessly in her mouth like a fish on the bottom of a boat. She'd had similar conversations with psychos and low-lifes before, but there was something about this man—a coldness, a remoteness—that frightened her.

"Excess," the voice said.

"What?"

"Excess," he repeated. "A six-letter word for 'more than enough.' Does it fit?"

"Yeah, it fits. Okay, I've got a few extra minutes. What's on your mind?"

"Be at the Silverado tonight at five-thirty."

"The Silverado? That's a country-western joint." She jotted "Silverado" and "5:30" on a notepad and showed it to Dan Logan. He shook his head. "Is this another 'exclusive,' or are you inviting *60 Minutes* along?"

"If you are there precisely at five-thirty, you will learn more."

"More about what?"

He hung up.

"Shit!" she spat, slamming the phone down.

"What's his story?" Dan asked.

Dahlia was about to tell him, but saw Carl Peoples leaning a curious ear toward them. "Your place," she said, ejecting the tape and marching Dan toward his office.

Peoples watched them talking animatedly through the glass. Casually he stood up and strolled by Dahlia's desk, reading the notepad: "Silverado, 5:30."

"What'll it be, honey?" the cocktail waitress asked Dahlia. The waitress wore a cowboy hat and blouse with fringes on the sleeves. She also wore spiked heels, black tights, and a red leotard with matching fringes circling her hips.

"Beer," Dahlia said.

"Light?" The waitress grinned.

"Sure. Can't hurt to watch those calories."

The waitress walked off, her fringes shimmering. Dahlia looked around at the other patrons, mostly men, with bottles and pitchers of beer crowding their small tables. There were a lot of cowboy boots in the place, she noticed. Some were old and muddy, some new and fancy. Some men wore jogging shoes, though the flabby guts hanging over their belts belied any actual running. Some wore thick steel-toed workboots that laced up over their shins. None looked like the kind of man who'd belong to that smooth, cold voice on the phone.

The few women in the place wore too much makeup and looked both weary and restless. Most were with men, but a few were in couples together, checking the men out. One women of about thirty was alone at the bar, trying unsuccessfully to light her cigarette.

"You look lonely," someone said behind Dahlia.

She turned around and saw a big man grinning at her. He was about forty, near six-foot-four, and not a pound under 250. He wore a sweat-stained cowboy hat and was reeling a little from too much drink. He grinned at her, holding up two bottles of beer.

"Thought you could use some company."

"I'm waiting for someone," she said.

"Well, I'm someone." He laughed, plopping down in the chair opposite her.

"Not to me. Now please leave."

"I just got here." He slammed one of the bottles in front of her. "Drink."

It was a very small table and his sour breath washed over her like a thick fog. More important, she was worried that his presence might frighten away whomever she was supposed to be meeting. She had to get rid of him.

The waitress arrived with her light beer.

"Hey, Linda," he said, tickling the fringes of her leotard. "I see by your outfit that you are a cowgirl."

"Yeah, well I smell by your breath that you are drunk. Go home." She brushed his thick hand away from her fringes.

"Put this lady's beer on my tab."

The waitress looked sympathetically at Dahlia. "You want me to have the bartender dump him?"

Still not wanting to draw any attention to herself that would chase away her informant, she shook her head. "Thanks. I'll handle it."

Linda shrugged and left.

Encouraged, the big cowboy leaned toward her. "You and me could have some fun."

"Not likely." Under the table, Dahlia quietly worked her hand into her purse, felt blindly through the contents. When she found the sharp nail file, she pulled it out and held it on her lap, waiting.

He leaned even closer. "I'm talking about some heavy passion, baby. Satisfaction guaranteed. Ain't many things that are guaranteed anymore in this fucking world." He covered her hand with his.

Dahlia used her other hand to poke the nail file under the table toward him. It jabbed lightly into his crotch and he jumped.

"Hey!"

"I've got a knife bumping up against your brain, buster. I suggest you take a hike or lose your 'satisfaction guaranteed' line forever."

The big man looked confused and nervous. Sweat dripped down the side of his nose.

"You okay, ma'am?" the bartender asked Dahlia from behind the bar. "You say the word and I'll toss Kravitz out on his butt."

Dahlia stared into Kravitz's eyes. He blinked rapidly, then stood up.

"No problem, Dave," Kravitz told the bartender soberly. "I'll finish my beers at the bar."

Finally alone, Dahlia looked at her watch. Almost five-thirty. Still no one approached her. She stood up, pretended to walk toward the rest rooms, casually surveying the patrons. There in the back, a man crouched in the corner. The little lantern at his table was blown out. She took a couple of steps toward him for a better look.

"Son of a bitch!" she muttered and marched straight for him. "Goddamn it, Peoples, what are you doing here?"

Peoples looked up innocently. "Hey, McGuire, what a coincidence."

"Jeez, you're slime."

"What do you mean? I come here all the time. That's my buck in the jukebox playing all those Willie Nelson songs."

Dahlia shook a warning finger at him. "You louse this up for me, Peoples, and I'll have you arrested on a morals charge. "

"I don't have any morals," Peoples said with a laugh. But he looked nervous.

Dahlia smiled. "You know I can do it. A call to a cop friend and they'll be hauling your ass into jail for molesting someone's pigs. I'll write the story for the paper myself."

Peoples didn't say anything. He just sat there and sipped his beer, brooding.

Dahlia spun away and was walking back to her table when the front door opened and a black man walked in. He wore a long purple brushed-velvet coat and matching wide-brimmed hat. White rabbit fur lined the lapels. He glanced around as if looking for someone. His dark eyes rested on Dahlia for a moment.

"Can't be," she muttered. "Talk about inconspicuous. Christ."

Suddenly Kravitz stood up from the bar and walked toward the black man. Kravitz looked over his shoulder at Dahlia, making sure she noticed him. He winked at her. When he was standing in front of the black man, he took a long slow look from head to toe and chuckled. "Hey, man, who's your tailor? The Merry Faggots of the West?"

The black man ignored Kravitz, looking past him at the other patrons, scanning the room.

"I'm talking to you, Jamaica. You come waltzin' in here with your pimp clothes, man. You ain't turnin' this place into no whore bar for niggers."

Dave the bartender came rushing around from behind the bar. He was as big as Kravitz, though not quite as heavy. He stepped between the two men. "Kravitz, shut up and get out. You've had enough."

"Christ, look at him, Dave."

"Go home." Dave turned to the black man. "Sorry, sir. Welcome to the Silverado. Come on in, have a drink on the house. Linda, take the gentleman's order."

The black man smiled a friendly smile and began unbuttoning his coat. When he'd finished, he reached inside and pulled out a Uzi submachine gun and opened fire.

Dave the bartender was hit first, his chest pounded to swampy pulp by a burst of 9mm bullets. Kravitz was too stunned to run; he caught the next burst in the stomach and dropped to his knees, trying to hold his guts in. He failed.

A second black man came through the door, his Uzi already drawn and firing. He took out the three patrons at the bar, including the drunken woman who'd passed out earlier.

Dahlia kicked over her tiny table and dove behind it. A couple of bullets chipped the top of the table off and she retracted her head lower into her neck. Around her she could hear the screams, see people being torn up by the bullets. Linda the cocktail waitress came running by and Dahlia reached out and grabbed her feet, bringing her tumbling to the floor. Then she dragged her behind the table.

To the left she saw Peoples crawling on all fours toward the women's rest room. A burst of bullets chewed up the linoleum floor in front of him, sending the sawdust jumping into the air. Another burst stitched along the floor like an invisible sewing machine, the bullets marching between People's legs and up his spine, nailing him to the floor.

Linda screamed at the sight, but Dahlia clamped a hand over her mouth.

Dahlia peeked around the table, saw the two men grimacing as they fired again and again.

"What'll we do?" Linda sobbed. "They'll kill us."

"Just wait. Hide. It's all we can do." Dahlia was trying to sound calm, but she didn't feel calm. She watched the bodies of the patrons flop helplessly, blood splashing everywhere.

A loud crash of shattering glass drowned out the clatter of Uzis for a moment. Dahlia sneaked a glance and saw the same impressive-looking man she'd seen a few days earlier where those kids in the car had been shot. Right now he was flying through the window, clutching a pump-action shotgun. He somersaulted across the glass-covered floor as the two black gunmen turned and sprayed bullets at him. The bullets chopped floor and glass and dead bodies, but missed the man with the shotgun as he flipped over, skipped to his feet, and fired two roaring blasts of the shotgun. The first shot slammed the second gunman into the wall, his head smashing a neon Miller High Life sign. The gunman in the long coat managed to dash out the door as Hunter's second shot peppered the wall behind him.

Dahlia watched their rescuer run to the doorway, pump three more rounds into the night, and curse at the sound of squealing tires racing away. He started out the door, but the wail of police sirens seemed to stop him. She watched him frown, could almost see him considering options. Suddenly he turned and marched back into the bar, straight toward her. He stopped at her table, looking down at Dahlia and the waitress. "Come on," he said.

"What do you mean?"

He sighed impatiently. "Come on."

Some of the wounded moaned. Those who hadn't been hit began crawling out from their hiding places.

"Who are you?" Dahlia asked him.

"Matt Hunter. Now let's go."

"Is this a kidnapping?"

Linda blurted out, "Please don't take us."

Hunter frowned. "This isn't a kidnapping. And I only want you, Ms. McGuire."

"You know me?"

The sirens were growing louder.

105

"This isn't the time for false modesty, lady. You want a story? I want something too. You want to deal?"

Dahlia studied his face. It was rugged, the nose a little crooked from being broken a few times. The eyes were distant, not giving anything away. She didn't know what to do, so she went with her instincts. "Yeah, okay." She stood up. "Where we going?"

"Out of here," he said. He grabbed her hand and pulled her along behind him.

"This had better be worth it," she said, stepping over the dead body of Carl Peoples.

"You talked to him, didn't you?" Hunter asked as he drove John Eagle's truck through the dark alleys of Miami.

"Talked to who?"

Hunter gave her a sour look. "Let's not play reporter right now, okay?"

"I'm not playing, Mr. Hunter. I am a reporter, as you damn well know. So don't play macho beefcake with me, okay?"

He looked over at her and grinned. "I am a macho beefcake."

Dahlia laughed—not with humor, but with relief. She hadn't realized just how frazzled her nerves were, how scared she'd been. She shoved her hands into her jacket so he wouldn't see them trembling. They felt like little birds fluttering in her pockets. She took a deep breath, thought of the dead: Peoples, Dave the bartender, Kravitz. She felt sorry for each of them.

"Relax," Hunter said. "They weren't trying to kill you. You were probably in the safest place in Miami back there."

"What the hell are you talking about? There are dead bodies all over that place."

"Did they shoot at you?"

"Yes. They took off the whole top of the table where I was hiding."

"Which kept you hunkered on the floor, out of the way of stray bullets."

"You're nuts."

"Nope. I just know the man we're dealing with. He probably called you, told you you'd get some kind of story if you showed up there. Right?"

Dahlia didn't answer. She stared out the windshield.

Hunter continued: "Like I said, he's smart. He may bomb everything from hospitals to post offices, but he never touches the media. That's how he spreads his brand of fear and panic. He uses you guys like toilet paper, then tosses you away."

"Nice image," Dahlia said coldly. "Maybe you should be the writer."

He patted the shotgun jammed between the seat and dashboard. "Right now this is the only communication that will make any difference. Things are only going to get worse."

"Who is this guy you're talking about? What's his name?"

"Off the record?"

She shook her head. "This is too important to go off the record."

"It won't do you any good anyway. There's no way you can verify what I tell you. You talk to the people who know and they'll claim they never heard of him or me."

"CIA?"

"Off the record?"

"How'd you know to be at the Silverado?"

"I followed you."

"You what?"

"I followed you. I knew our friend would be contacting the top reporters and sending them somewhere where they could witness a media event. I'm sure there are half a dozen other reporters and camera crews at various locations in Miami right now recording a spontaneous outburst of violence between two racially diverse groups. That's how he always stages it."

"Who?"

"Off the record?" Hunter repeated.

"Damn!" She glared at him. "Yeah, off the record."

"His name is Mikal Rostov. Trained by the Soviet Union, he's their top specialist on terrorism and revolution. Give him ten minutes in a baby nursery and he'll have infants armed and demanding softer diapers. The man's a genius. He's also a homocidal maniac."

"Quite a combination. What's he doing here?"

"Invading the U.S. Give him two more weeks and he'll have destroyed the economic structure of this whole country. Hold up people's pay checks and they'll get mad. Give them a group to get mad at, a reason to hate, and they'll attack. He's got the blacks and whites killing each other off. Not to mention Cubans and cops, Nazis and Jews. A couple more days and no one will trust anyone else. We'll all be shooting at everybody."

"Those black men at the bar. They were Russians?"

"Afro-Cubans, probably. They're darker skinned. Did they say anything?"

"No."

Hunter nodded. "That's because they probably only speak Spanish."

108

"Jesus." She let out a long, weary sigh. "They might just pull it off."

"Yeah," Hunter agreed.

"What do you want with me?"

"I need you on the inside. When and if Rostov calls again, I need you to tell me immediately. The only way to stop this is to get rid of him and his henchmen. If I can get to the scene of one of these staged outbursts, I might be able to take a prisoner, find out where Rostov is."

"What if he doesn't call me?"

"I'm working on another source. That's where I'm going now. Right after I drop you off. Paper okay?"

Dahlia nodded. "Yeah, sure."

Hunter wheeled the pickup around the corner onto Alton Road, heading south toward the General MacArthur Causeway.

"You notice the sound?" Dahlia said. "Sirens. I've been hearing them all night."

"Better get used to it."

Dahlia stared out into the darkness, squinting. The headlights, streetlights, office building lights all became fuzzy splotches of white. UFOs or luminous cotton balls. Sometimes when things got bad she would do that and feel better. The lights were something else, something wonderful and exciting. This time it didn't work. She opened her eyes again and saw the city lights, heard the screaming sirens. "I'm going with you."

"Wrong," Hunter said firmly.

"No, I mean it. You want my help, I want yours."

"I saved your life back in that cowboy bar."

"According to you I wasn't really in danger."

Hunter grinned. "You catch on."

"And I'm going with you."

"I'll take you there, but you can't come inside. They'd chew you up in there. There would be nothing left of you but some plaque on their teeth and dirt under their fingernails."

"You trying to scare me?"

"Damn right."

"I'm still going." Dahlia crossed her arms.

"Okay," Hunter said. "But don't expect me to pull any macho beefcake number and help you. I'm after information."

"Fine."

They sat in silence as Hunter drove down a few more dark alleys.

"Why me?" she finally asked. "Why'd you follow me?"

"Rostov had tipped you once, I figured he was bound to do it again. You are a top reporter in the city."

"Thanks."

"Also, you're easy to follow in that dumb jeep of yours."

She was about to say something when he pulled the pickup over and announced, "We're here."

"Here where?" she said, looking around the dark alley.

"The bar I told you about."

"What bar? There's no sign or anything."

"That's the kind of bar it is. If you don't know where it is, you're not welcome. Sometimes you're not welcome anyway."

"Great," she said, climbing out of the truck. "Who hangs out here?"

"Lots of people. Bikers, dopers, ex-cons. Mercenaries mostly. This is kind of like their union hall. They wait here between jobs."

"You know the nicest people."

Hunter locked the truck and led the way into the shadows. She followed after him, but couldn't see anything but blackness where he was walking. Suddenly he reached into a shadow and yanked on something. A door creaked open and a sliver of light and smoke sliced through the darkness. Creedence Clearwater Revival's "Bad Moon Rising" filtered out into the night.

"Let's go," Hunter said, walking in ahead of her.

The bar was like some middle-class nightmare of hell. Through the thick bitter smoke and the sour smell of sweat, huge hulking men sat or stood, each clutching a drink. Their faces were all different, but their expressions were the same: hollow eyes, grim mouths. The women were mostly lean and lanky and just as predatory-looking. They glared at the two newcomers with primal hostility that reminded Hunter of the alligators he hunted.

"Stay close," Hunter said to Dahlia.

"Damn right," she replied.

Hunter smiled to himself. This woman was tough in a way these tattooed, leather-clad women would never be. She was bright and articulate and talented, yet she obviously cared about other people. And she was willing to risk her life to help. Sure, she was agressive and ambitious, but Hunter admired that in her.

"I've never seen so many scars," Dahlia whispered.

"They probably got most of them fighting each other in joints like this. Mercenary work is very seasonal. They get restless."

"They look a little restless right now."

"They are." Hunter peered through the smoke, looking for the man he thought could help him. Whether he would or not, Hunter didn't know. Last time they'd met, they'd parted on good terms. But there had been other times, other wars, when they hadn't been on the same side. That was one good thing about mercs, though; they didn't hold a grudge about such things.

A too-skinny woman wearing nothing but a silver-spangled bikini bottom was dancing listlessly on the bar. She bumped her hips back and forth out of sync with the music, staring off into the smoke as if she were someplace else. A big burly man with an American-flag eyepatch stood in front of her, leering and grinning. Occasionally he would reach up and stuff a dollar bill into her panties, his fingers lingering. She didn't seem to notice or care.

When she saw Hunter, her interest suddenly picked up. She danced awkwardly along the bar until she was standing in front of him and Dahlia, looking down. "Hey, Hunter."

"Hi, Connie."

"Who's the squeeze? Very chichi."

"Connie, this is Dahlia."

"Hi," Connie said, still gyrating her hips.

"Hi." Dahlia nodded, staring at the thin scar that ran from Connie's knee up her thigh and disappeared under the leg of her panties.

The music from the jukebox stopped, but Connie kept on dancing. Another song started up, the Rolling Stones' "Brown Sugar." Connie's dancing was slightly more in rhythm with this song, but only accidentally.

"Seen Flynn?" Hunter asked.

"He's here. Other end of the bar. C'mon, I'll show you." She started to dance along the bar, Hunter and Dahlia following alongside. Until the man with the

112

American-flag eyepatch wrapped a boulder-sized hand around Connie's ankle.

"I been pumping dollar bills into your slot all night, chick," he growled. "I'm not paying you to grind your pussy in someone else's face."

"Fuck off, Palance," Connie said, trying to shake her ankle free.

Hunter sighed. He didn't want a fight; he just wanted information. He felt the others in the room tensing, watching. They were all getting ready to brawl, waiting for an excuse to punch the person at the table next to them or even the guy they'd been drinking with all night. They had the mean, hungry look of junkyard dogs.

"We're just old friends," Hunter explained quietly to Palance. "I knew her brother."

Palance scowled at Hunter, leaning his bulk and height over the smaller man. "I don't give a fuck if you and him were faggot lovers. Those are my bucks in her panties, and if she don't want to dance, I want 'em back."

"Here," Connie said, plucking dollar bills like feathers. She tossed a handful into Palance's face.

He grinned. "Now I want interest." He reached up and grabbed her panties in his fist, yanking hard. The panties ripped free, silver spangles flying everywhere.

Connie stood there completely naked, but didn't try to cover herself. She placed one hand on her hip and shook a finger in Palance's bearded face. "Look what you've done, you dumb ox. That was my last pair with all the spangles. You know how much spangles cost? They gotta be sewed on individually. Shit!"

Dahlia elbowed Hunter aside, snatched the handful of bills from Palance's fist, and handed them to Connie. "Here, Connie. He tore it, he can pay for it."

Palance turned his huge head toward Dahlia. He looked at her trim body and licked his lips. ''Maybe you'd like to take her place, honey?'' And with a quick movement, he lifted Dahlia up onto the bar, grabbed the hem of her skirt, and tore it straight up one pantyhosed thigh. Hoots of approval echoed from the other patrons.

''Leave her alone,'' Connie shouted, kicking at Palance's face. Her toe brushed his eyepatch, shifting it slightly, enough to reveal the thick scaly scar tissue where his eye used to be.

''Damn,'' Hunter muttered. ''A quiet chat, that's all I wanted.''

Palance was about to rip Dahlia's dress farther when Hunter reached over, grabbed a handful of wiry beard, and jerked the big man's head around. Instantly he snapped the palm of his hand between Palance's eyes, stunning him. While Palance was still dazed, Hunter pulled the merc's hand up and put him in a thumb-and-finger lock, applying just enough pressure so that both fingers were on the brink of breaking at the joints.

Palace yowled with pain and dropped to his knees.

Hunter shook his head. ''Now this here is a dangerous hold and should only be attempted by professionals. Don't any of you in the home audience try this.''

''I'll kill you, asshole,'' Palance screamed through the pain.

''You'll try,'' Hunter said, reaching over to the bar for Palance's half-full mug of beer. He raised the mug as if to clobber Palance, hesitated, brought it to his mouth, then drank the beer in one gulp. He smacked his lips and smashed Palance on the head with the empty mug. The glass shattered, leaving only the handle in Hunter's hand. Palance sagged to the floor, unconscious.

114

Hunter looked up at Dahlia. "Well, either dance or come on down." He reached up to help her. She leaned into his arms and his hands felt her warm flesh beneath the clothing. As he lifted her down, a waft of exotic perfume stung his nose pleasantly. Her face was only inches from his now, her long hair slightly mussed, her eyes deep and intelligent, always thinking.

"Thanks," she said. "This time you really did save my life."

For the rest of the patrons the moment of violence had passed. Palance's humiliation wasn't enough to make them want to fight. There was still plenty of time for that. The night was young.

"Gotta go fix my costume," Connie said, taking off toward the stool at the end of the bar. "See ya, Hunter. Thanks, Dahlia."

"Bye, Connie," Dahlia said.

Hunter stepped over Palance's sleeping body and proceeded down the bar until he saw the man he'd been looking for. "Your turn to buy, isn't it, Flynn?"

Flynn flashed three fingers at the bartender. "Three beers, George."

"How's business?"

"It's been better. Economy's down. Lots of amateurs running around out there reading *Soldier of Fortune*, thinking all they need's a gun, a camouflage hat, and a moustache and they're in business. Unfortunately, they're pulling the price down."

"You don't look too worried."

Flynn shrugged. "I'm flush for now. Managed to pick up a nice short-term contract in Thailand."

"Be sure to mention my name over there."

Flynn snorted. "Not if I want to keep breathing. Any-

115

way, the way things are starting to look, I may find some work right here at home. Save a fortune on air fares.''

George, the bartender, set the beers down, slopping some over the rims of the mugs. Flynn handed him a crisp twenty. George nodded and left. For the first time, Flynn looked past Hunter at Dahlia. Then he turned to Hunter. ''At least you're keeping better company than last time I saw you.''

''Strictly business.''

''Business, huh? I thought you were out of the spook business.''

Hunter fixed Flynn with a hard look. ''Rostov's back.''

Flynn stopped in mid-sip, blinked, then continued drinking his beer. He wiped his mouth with the back of his hand, then ran his fingers through his curly steel-gray hair. ''Bad penny, that one. You should have killed him when you had the chance.''

Hunter sipped his beer silently.

''You think he's behind all this?'' Flynn continued.

''Who else?''

''Yeah, it's his style all right. You gotta give that much to the asshole. He's efficient.''

''I've got to find him, Flynn.''

Flynn looked over at Dahlia. ''You talk or what?''

Dahlia started to speak, but Hunter cut her off. ''She's not in this part. This is between you and me.''

''Christ, Hunter.'' Flynn grinned. ''You never did have any patience. You're supposed to butter me up first. Offer me a bribe or something.''

''You give me something solid, I'll make a call. You'll have a contract by morning and the start of a South American tan by afternoon.''

Flynn stared into his beer for a few moments, scratched

his head. "I don't know if this is anything, but I saw some new faces last night over at the Corazon d'Oro."

"What kind of new faces?" Hunter asked.

"Experienced faces. Like they know which way to duck when a grenade goes off. Only I've never seen them before. That's unusual. Maybe it's something, maybe not."

Hunter stood up and patted Flynn on the back. "I'll make the call."

Flynn nodded, lifted his beer in a toast. "See ya in hell."

"Maybe," Hunter said. "But I'll be the one passing through."

"Where to now?" Dahlia asked as Hunter drove the pickup out of the alley.

"Corazon d'Oro."

"What's that?"

"Kind of a combination whorehouse, saloon, doper den. Makes this place look like a country club."

"Christ, Hunter, you sure know how to take a girl out on the town."

"I guess I'm just an old-fashioned romantic."

Dahlia laughed as she plucked several silver spangles from her jacket.

11

"This is wrong, man," Gibbons protested. "Rostov left strict orders."

"Rostov is an old woman sometimes," Tomas said.

Gibbons looked around nervously as if he thought Rostov might be hiding in the empty alley. Gibbons had been building bombs since his old Columbia University days with the Weathermen. With the FBI nipping at his ass, he'd sneaked into Canada, then down to Cuba. From there he'd gone to terrorist training camps in Libya and South America. Now three months short of forty, Gibbons had lost his political zeal somewhere along the way. In the darkest part of the night, when he woke up sweating and chilled, he admitted that he no longer considered himself a political activist, merely a professional terrorist, a paid demolitions expert, like a guy on a construction site. Still, in his travels from terrorist group to terrorist group, the name of Rostov was spoken with awe and fear. Everyone had a story about Rostov, a gruesome story of cruelty and evil. But Tomas was young and brash, a lot like Gibbons had been back in his fiery SDS days, when staying in bed with a woman was just as important as staying outside the Establishment. Now staying alive was all that seemed important.

"One drink," Gibbons agreed, "that's all."

"I didn't come here for a drink. I came for a woman." Tomas winked. "You should try it sometime."

"Rostov told us to stay put."

Tomas waved a dismissing hand. The hand was wrapped in a thick white dressing to protect the wound from Hunter's bullet. "Rostov, Rostov, Rostov. I didn't realize how easily you Americans frighten. Remember the Alamo, my friend, and *High Noon*. Be strong like Gary Cooper." Tomas laughed. "Even the great Rostov has acted foolishly, chasing after the man Hunter. One full day we wasted for his crazy obsession, and it cost me this." He held up the bandaged hand.

"Quiet," Gibbons said. Speaking of Rostov this way was like blasphemy, Gibbons thought. If anyone overheard and word got back to Rostov, there would be great pain involved before the welcomed death.

The two men emerged onto a street that was just as dark and filthy as the alley, only slightly wider. There, next to the boarded-up windows of what had once been a dry cleaner's, was a flickering neon sign that read CORAZON D'ORO. The sign buzzed like an angry wasp.

In front of the building was the Corazon d'Oro's giant bouncer, Victor, waxing his red 1964 Cadillac El Dorado. Each stroke from his redwood-thick arm was a loving caress, a labor of devotion. Everything about the sleek convertible exuded loving care. The whitewalls gleamed, even in the night. The chrome caught the flicker of the red neon light, making it look like molten fire wrapped around the car. The interior was a pink fur, thick as cotton candy. Orange and black lightning bolts were hand-painted across each sweeping fin.

"How's it going?" Tomas waved as they passed the car.

Victor glared as if suspecting they were here to steal his prize. His large pumpkin head didn't move as he continued rubbing the wax into an already immaculate sheen. But his eyes followed them each step of the way.

"Maybe we should wait for Hector," Gibbons suggested. Hector was parking their car a few blocks away just in case Rostov might pass by.

"He'll find us," Tomas said.

The two men entered the building.

Gibbons searched the crowd nervously, checking for Rostov even though he knew the Russian was in the field assassinating a Vietnamese refugee family and leaving evidence blaming a veterans' group.

Tomas grinned, licked his lips, and began moving with the music, an old Iron Butterfly song Gibbons remembered from his college days. The smoke was as thick as a battlefield, and some of it had the sweet pungency of marijuana. In a corner booth, a couple of guys were snorting a line of cocaine, rubbing the crumbs on their gums.

Gibbons sighed. Most of the crowd was Cuban, but there was a sprinkling of blacks and whites. Everyone had one thing in common: they all lived on the underbelly of society. Gibbons remembered the biology class he'd flunked out of because he'd been too busy attending rallies. One time, though, they'd discussed the remora, that little fish that attaches itself to the shark and eats the leftovers.

That's what these people were like, only they saw themselves as the shark.

A fight broke out at the bar. The bartender hauled a baseball bat out and clubed the man closest to him. The fight was over. He rang a ship's bell over the bar and Victor came in, lifted the unconscious man up, and threw him out the door into the street. Then he went back to waxing his car.

Hookers of all shapes, sizes, ages, and colors wove through the crowd like the smoke. Gibbons's interest in women had subsided slightly because of the numerous venereal diseases he'd picked up. They'd taken a toll. Tomas, however, was grinding up against each one, laughing, pawing, whispering. One small hooker, nineteen at most, sidled up to Tomas, elbowing another older woman out of the way.

"You come back to see Carmen, huh?" She grinned.

Tomas laughed. "No, but you'll do." He grabbed her hand and started pulling her through the crowd toward the stairs that led to the rooms.

"You'd better make it quick," Gibbons said. "We don't have much time."

"I never make it quick," Tomas said. "Eh, Carmen?"

"Never," Carmen said.

The two of them squeezed through the crowd. As Carmen hopped up the stairs, the light hit her dress just right, and Gibbons could see she wasn't wearing any underwear.

"Not bad stuff," Hector said, walking up to Gibbons.

"Where's the car?"

"Hidden. Don't worry."

Both men watched Carmen climb the last few stairs. For two seconds they were able to stare up her mini-skirt and confirm Gibbons's judgment. They looked at each other.

"What the hell." Hector shrugged. "We're here. We might as well get laid."

Gibbons nodded. "I'll just watch."

"Fine, but you still have to pay half."

"Okay."

They shoved through the crowd on the stairs. Along the way, Hector snagged a willing woman.

Tomas let her unbutton his shirt while he squeezed her nipples through her dress. She smiled up at him.

"I think that last beer is knocking to come out again," she said. Her Spanish was strictly downtown Havana, he realized. "Get ready, baby, I'll be right back."

He gave her nipples a hard pinch that caused her to wince. "Hurry."

She forced a smile back on her face and nodded. She hurried out the door to the bathroom down the hall.

Tomas continued working at his buttons, but it was difficult because of his bandaged hand. Frustrated, he finally pulled the shirt over his head, gritting his teeth at the pain in his hand. He was almost sorry Hunter was dead. He would have liked to kill him again for what he'd done to his hand. He unbuckled his belt and tugged at his zipper.

Footsteps pattered outside the door.

Tomas smiled. "I hope you are hungry, Carmenita. Hurry and see what I have for your dinner."

The door exploded open, swinging into the wall with a crash.

Hunter stood framed in the doorway. His smile was grim, like something acid might have etched in concrete.

"Shit!" Tomas said, swallowing hard.

Hunter took a step toward him and Tomas staggered back a few steps, bumping into the wall.

Suddenly Hunter heard the pounding steps behind him and spun just as Hector and Gibbons dove through the door and tackled him to the ground. A fist slammed into his stomach and another crunched his ear. Out of the corner of his eye, Hunter could see Tomas sliding along the wall toward the exit. He had to move fast or he'd lose his only chance at finding Rostov.

Not much different than alligators, Hunter thought as he stabbed his elbow into Gibbons's eye, just more arms and legs to deal with. Gibbons fell back, holding his already swollen eye. Hunter rolled away from Hector, jumped to his feet, and executed a spinning back kick to Tomas's chest that knocked him into the wall with a thud. Tomas sagged a little, trying to catch his breath.

Hector was on his feet now, directly behind Hunter. He swung his knee into Hunter's kidney. Hunter groaned from the impact but immediately pivoted, grabbed a handful of Hector's curly black hair, and ran him face first into the wall. Hector's nose popped like a brown banana. Blood speckled the dingy wall. Hector sank to the floor unconscious.

But Gibbons was ready. He flipped out his Philippine butterfly knife, flicking his wrist so the double handle opened to reveal the deadly blade inside. He lunged at Hunter's stomach.

Hunter sidestepped one thrust, then another. The third attack was a powerful disemboweling swipe that nicked Hunter's shirt and a sixteenth of an inch of skin. He felt the warm blood well up along the gash in his stomach.

Hunter concentrated on Gibbons's attacks, even though he saw Tomas slowly moving for the door again. There was nothing he could do about it right now. The man with the knife knew what he was doing.

Gibbons faked a slash and Hunter fell for it, jumping back against the wall. But instead of the slash, Gibbons thrust the blade straight at Hunter's face. Hunter pulled away just before the blade gouged a hole in the wall, sticking deep in the plaster.

Hunter snapped his own forehead straight into Gibbons's face, dazing him. Gibbons released his grasp on the knife and stumbled backwards. Three jabs to the head followed by a side kick to the temple finished him off.

Tomas was almost at the door when Hunter yanked the knife out of the plaster and threw it across the room. The knife drilled through Tomas's wounded hand, pinning it to the wall. He yowled with pain, tears of fear and agony mixing as he frantically tugged at the knife, trying to free himself.

"Shouldn't play with knives," Hunter said, backhanding Tomas in the face. The terrorist thumped back into the wall, his hand still impaled there. Blood was soaking through the white gauze of his bandage.

"What do you want?" he yelled.

"Rostov," Hunter said quietly.

"I don't know where he is. I swear."

"Maybe all the excitement has given you a memory lapse. Let's see if we can stimulate your brain a little." Hunter jabbed his palm into the pommel of the knife, driving it deeper into the terrorist's hand.

Tomas cried out.

Hunter whispered, "Rostov."

"I don't know, man. No one knows exactly. He's always on the move. Everywhere. Nowhere."

Hunter grabbed the pommel. "Sometimes I like to pre-

tend I'm in a sports car shifting gears. There's first . . ."
He pushed the knife upwards as if it were a gear shift.

"I swear," Tomas pleaded.

"Second . . ." Hunter pulled the knife backwards.

"Please!"

"I can't wait for reverse."

"Jesus!"

Hunter heard the heavy pounding of running feet coming down the hall. Carmen's screechy voice was yelling in Spanish, "Hurry. They're in the last room. Hurry!"

Hunter unzipped the breast pocket of his down vest and pulled out an M26 hand grenade. It was olive green with big yellow lettering that said: HANDGRENADE, FRAG M26, COMP B. He clamped his teeth on the pin and jerked it out, then slapped the grenade into Tomas's free hand.

Tomas gripped it tightly, his knuckles white with effort. "What are you doing? You're crazy, man. Fuckin' crazy!"

Victor, Carmen, and another ox-sized bouncer stood in the doorway. The two men's huge bodies boxed out any light from the hallway.

"What the fuck are you guys doing?" Victor asked.

"You sure you want to know?" Hunter said, stepping away from Tomas.

Victor saw the knife pinning Tomas's left hand to the wall. Then he saw the pinless grenade in his right hand.

"Help me," Tomas demanded.

Victor shrugged. "Settle it yourselves." He tapped his partner on the shoulder and they started to walk away. Carmen blew a kiss to Tomas and followed the two bouncers down the hall.

Hunter smiled at Tomas. "I hate drop-in visitors, don't you?"

"Give me a break, man. Come on."

Hunter grabbed the pommel.

"All right! I don't know where Rostov is, but I know where we were hitting next. The shopping mall out on Arthur Godfrey Road."

Hunter headed for the door.

"It's too late," Tomas said. "I was supposed to be there by now. That place is history, man. Nothing but blood and dust."

Hunter stopped, looked back at Tomas. "Just in case you see Rostov before I do, tell him to check his watch. It's time to die."

Hunter ran out of the room. He knew Victor and the others would be waiting for him downstairs, so he needed another way out. The fire escape bolted to the side of the building emptied out into the alley that led to Dahlia McGuire and the truck. It had gotten him in unnoticed; it should get him out too.

Hunter heard Tomas's cries for help as he ducked into one of the bedrooms that had access to the fire escape. The man and woman were still naked in bed, still unconscious, just as he'd left them on his way in. There wasn't much Tomas could do right now. The window was on the same wall to which his hand was pinned. It would take some incredible contortions to toss the grenade outside.

Hunter scrambled down the metal fire escape. When he got to the lowest platform, he didn't want to risk the noise the ladder would probably make, so he hung over the side and dropped to the ground. A jolt of pain shot through his ankle where the alligator had nipped him a few days earlier. But that was back when John Eagle had still been alive. When the majority of Americans had been happy, almost smug in their feelings of safety. Before the bombings and riots and hate and suspicion.

Hunter crept to the edge of the building and peeked around the corner. Victor and the other bouncer were leaning against his pink Caddy, each holding a sawed-off shotgun, waiting for him.

The sound of breaking glass overhead disrupted their wait. Both men looked up and saw the dark grenade come plummeting through the air toward them.

Hunter grinned. Tomas had managed to make the window after all. It must have cost him some severe pain.

The grenade seemed almost to float for a moment, dropping silently through the night. Victor and his partner dove away from the car and rolled across the pavement toward a row of battered trash cans.

The grenade plopped into the pink fur-lined driver's seat and exploded. The Caddy blew apart in a fiery shower of red metal and pink fur.

"Son of a bitch!" Victor screamed, running over to his flaming car, pacing helplessly around it. Finally in frustration, he aimed his shotgun and fired two rounds into the engine.

"Well?" Dahlia asked Hunter as he jumped into the pickup truck. She floored the pedal, and they screeched away. "What happened?"

"The usual," Hunter said. He gave her directions to the shopping mall. It would take ten minutes. He studied the people on the streets that they passed. Everyone looked like Rostov. He leaned back in the seat and closed his eyes. Rostov smiled at him. He opened his eyes and looked at Dahlia. "Hurry," he said, though he knew she couldn't drive any faster.

12

Kurt waited patiently behind the father and daughter. They couldn't decide on a gift for the missus. Kurt smiled to himself and looked at his watch. In a few minutes they'd be able to stop worrying about such trivialities forever.

"What's this called?" the father asked the young salesgirl.

"Midnight Mist," she replied. "It's very popular."

"Well, if it's all that popular, then I guess I shouldn't get it. Wouldn't want her smelling like everybody else, would I? Huh?" He laughed.

"Oh, Dad," the daughter said. She was about eighteen, the same age as the salesgirl. She and the salesgirl exchanged smiles to acknowledge they would never get as corny in their old age as he was.

"What's this?" He sniffed another bottle.

"Suspicion," the daughter said.

"Yeah, well, it smells suspicious. Like something from the bottom of a litter box."

Both girls giggled and the father laughed.

Kurt was losing his patience. He checked his watch again, then looked down at the big white Sears shopping bag clutched in his right hand. He could see the box wrapped in gold metallic paper, the bright red bow. Inside, he could imagine the digital timer flashing off numbers, getting closer to the moment of detonation.

Kurt had made many bombs in his career with Baader-Meinhof, but this was his best creation yet. Practically a work of art. Better even than the whistle bomb he'd used on the Offenbach traffic police. That time he'd exchanged three whistles with three he'd fixed by prying the halves apart, filling each half one-fourth full with an extremely friction-sensitive explosive, then replacing the ball with one coated with sandpaper. The first cop to use it had lost most of her jaw. They found her tongue on the sidewalk. The other two had been stopped in time.

And this bomb was even better. The American Gibbons had showed him how to extract the oxygen from alcohol, then replace it with metal arsenic to produce cacodyl, which explodes the moment it's exposed to air. The explosion is bad enough, but the bonus comes from the dense white smoke that accompanies the blast. White arsenic. One whiff would cause death within seconds.

The placing of the bomb had been strategically worked out. It had to be right here at the cosmetics counter. Right where the Sears store opened onto the rest of the mall. The explosion and gas would cause some damage, but the terror that followed was sure to cause even more. People would be stampeding each other as they ran for the exits. The parking lot would be the site for one accident after another. Few would return to this mall again, or to any of the malls, afraid of where the bombs might next go off. And the clever part was that bombs like this were going off in malls all over the country tonight. From now on, no one would be spending money, no one would be making money. The chain reaction would severely rattle the economy. Kurt grinned at the thought of using capitalism against itself.

But first he had to plant the bomb. And soon.

"What else ya got? Ya got anything that smells kinda like lilacs?"

"My God no." The daughter winced. "That's for old ladies on buses. Mom wants something sexy."

"Your mom's plenty sexy as she is."

"Yeah, we know that. But we've got to make *her* know that."

The father looked at his daughter, touched her cheek gently, and smiled. "When'd you get so smart?"

"When you weren't looking." She kissed him on the cheek. "Come on, let's check out some of those nightgowns over there." She took his hand and pulled him after her.

Relieved, Kurt stepped up to the counter.

"Yes, sir?" the salesgirl asked. "May I help you?" She scratched at a Band-aid on the crook of her arm.

"Hurt yourself?" Kurt asked, flashing a friendly smile. He set his Sears bag down, slowly nudging it with his foot toward the recess under the counter.

"No. A bunch of us gave blood today. Christmas and all. They expect a lot of traffic accidents, so they'll need extra blood."

"That was very kind of you." He was pleased that he spoke with hardly an accent.

"Well, to tell you the truth, at first I just volunteered to get out of work. Sears paid us for the time. But afterwards, when they were feeding us juice and cookies, I guess I felt pretty good. Christmasy, you know?''

"Yes, I know." He pointed to the display of perfumes. "Do you have Fascination?''

"Fascination? I never heard of that. Isn't it a song or something?''

"It's a perfume too. The only kind my wife will wear.''

The salegirl shook her head. "Sorry.''

"Thanks anyway. I'll check somewhere else.'' Kurt walked slowly away, a small grin playing at his lips. It would take two minutes to reach the mall exit. Just about the time the bomb would detonate.

Kurt walked out of the store into the mall area. The corridors were crowded with shoppers and displays of old dragsters from the 1950s and '60s. The cars were all shiny, with wild paint jobs. Placards with each car's history sat on their hoods. Kurt looked around, spotted his three comrades, and nodded to them. Without any acknowledgment, they turned and began walking quickly toward the far exit. Where was Tomas? He was supposed to be here too. Rostov would deal with him later. Right now it was most important to leave the area as quickly as possible. Kurt picked up his pace.

"Hey, mister!'' the voice called behind him. "You forgot your package.''

Startled, Kurt turned, saw the father hurrying toward him, holding up the Sears shopping bag.

Kurt shoved through the crush of Christmas shoppers. Over his shoulder he saw the father gaining on him.

"Hey! Your bag. Hey, buddy.''

Kurt felt the cold sweat popping out on his forehead as he clawed past people, his knees knocking into their bags. He pushed aside one little boy, who fell and began crying.

"Watch it, asshole," a man said to Kurt.

Kurt kept going. He squeezed past the shiny copper fountain that showed Juan Ponce de León in full battle regalia kneeling and sipping from the water, his copper face molded into an expression of bliss as if indeed he had finally found the Fountain of Youth he'd sought in 1513 and 1521. The designer wanted shoppers to feel that they too had found the Fountain of Youth right here at the mall.

"Mister!" the father shouted in exasperation. "I'm returning something, for Chrissake, not stealing it. Hold up."

Kurt waved at his three henchmen and they bullied their way through the packed shoppers to join him. The three of them fanned out in front of him like linemen punching a hole for their quarterback. But the crowd was too thick, the father too close. And time was running out.

All four men stopped, pulled out their Ingram Model 10 submachine guns, spun, and opened fire on the crowd. The .45 ACP slugs chopped through the shoppers, sending them sprawling into one another. Screams drowned out the mechanical clatter of the guns. Some shoppers fell wounded, some ran, others threw themselves on the ground.

However it was, a path cleared through the crowd like toppled dominoes. And there was the father, standing next to the fountain, the Sears bag in his hand.

Kurt aimed and fired a short burst into the man's chest.

The impact spun the father around, knocking him into the fountain next to Juan Ponce de León. The package floated on top of the water.

"Daddy!" the man's daughter cried and ran toward him.

Kurt looked at his watch.

Three . . .

Two . . .

One . . .

The explosion showered the crowd with water and slivers of spinning copper as lethal as tiny propellers. The thick white cloud that billowed out from the fountain spread out over the nearby shoppers, and soon gagging coughs could be heard. A few began to swoon, convulsing on the floor.

"Kurt!" one of the terrorists yelled.

Kurt turned, saw the two security guards running around the corner of the Nut House, guns drawn. They were trying to aim, but the panicky crowd kept running in front of them.

"Get down!" they hollered, but the frightened patrons didn't listen.

Kurt slapped in a fresh thirty-round magazine and opened fire. His three comrades did the same. The swarm of bullets buzzed through the crowd like a lawnmower, hacking down everyone between the terrorists and the security guards and then even the guards.

Kurt gestured with his head. "Let's go betore the fumes drift this way."

They nodded in agreement and closed ranks, each man covering a different direction as they jogged toward the huge glass entrance that rose forty feet up. Above the row of doors was a stained-glass portrait of General Andrew Jackson's capture of Pensacola that led to the cession of Florida to the United States.

"Tonio," Kurt called to the lead terrorist. "Go ahead and get the door."

Tonio nodded and jogged ahead. But as he peered out through the smoky gray glass, he saw a dark vehicle racing down the parking lot between the rows of cars, not slowing as it hurtled toward the door.

Tonio tried to speak a warning and lift his gun at the same time. But he was too late doing both.

John Eagle's pickup truck crashed through the doors, ripping out the metal frames and glass. The cool air-conditioned mall air swooshed into the warm night. Hunter was behind the wheel, pushing Dahlia McGuire's head down toward the floorboard.

The pickup swerved just in time to clip Tonio and catapult him through the display window of The Fashion Jungle. Glass shattered across the shiny mall floor as the terrorist flopped into the expensively clothed mannequins. A long dagger of window pierced his back and pushed up through his stomach, exiting just below the navel. The glass was smeared with blood and bits of intestines the size of flies.

Hunter aimed the car straight at the others and they scattered, diving for cover. Kurt managed to squeeze off a short burst from his Ingram, drilling a line of holes across the front fender.

Dahlia popped up from behind the dashboard and snapped four rapid photos.

"I told you to stay down," Hunter said, pushing her back.

"Then why'd you bring me?"

"To drive." He grinned. Then he flipped the door open, lifted the H&K MP-5 SD-3 SMG from his lap, and leaped from the cab, gun clacking away.

The pickup kept rolling straight down the middle of the mall. Driverless.

"Jesus!" Dahlia said, quickly sliding behind the wheel.

She stomped the gas pedal and rocketed past the terrorists and Hunter alike, zooming by some of her favorite stores.

Hunter crouched next to the broken window of The Fashion Jungle and sprayed the running terrorists with 9mm parabellums. One of them clutched his face and went down screaming. He died before hitting the ground.

Most of the shoppers had ducked into other stores or, too petrified to move, just pressed themselves to the walls or floor. Kurt and his henchman ducked around a corner just as a line of Hunter's bullets bit at their heels. Huddled there against the wall were two frightened teenage girls. Kurt grabbed the first one around the neck and yanked her to her feet. "What's your name?" he demanded.

She tried to speak, but the words choked in her throat.

Kurt shot her in the chest and threw her to the ground. The second girl, splattered with her dead friend's blood, screamed. Kurt dragged her to her feet. "What's your name?"

"D-D-Debbie," she sobbed.

Kurt held her in front of him as a shield and stepped back around the corner. But no Hunter.

"Hunter!" Kurt shouted.

No reply.

"Hunter, we have a hostage."

No answer.

Kurt jammed his gun under her chin, forcing her head back. "Come out now, Hunter, or she dies." Now his German accent was thick and guttural.

A long silence followed. The pickup truck at the other end of the mall had turned around and was idling, waiting.

"Come out, Hunter!" Kurt hollered. "Or we'll shoot her."

"Then shoot her." Hunter's voice bounced down the

corridor, but he was still out of sight. "But once she's dead, so are you."

Kurt pulled her even closer, his eyes flicking from store to store, looking for Hunter.

"Please . . ." Debbie pleaded.

Sweat drifted down Kurt's forehead, stinging his eyes. He blotted his face with a sleeve. "Listen, Hunter. Her name's Debbie. Such a sweet all-American name. Debbie is very sad right now. She just lost her best friend to an unfortunate accident . . ."

"Oh God!" Debbie sobbed.

Kurt drove his gun hard against her chin, cutting her off. "Shut up, Debbie. I'm bargaining for your life."

"No deals," Hunter's calm voice proclaimed. "I want Rostov. That's your only chance to live."

"You underestimate me, my friend. It is Rostov who fears you, not me." Kurt clutched Debbie closer to himself, then began slowly moving toward one of the dragsters on display. It was an old Chevy truck, circa 1950, with chrome headers coming out of the hood. It was painted a glossy black with red and yellow flames sweeping back over the doors. The bed of the truck was lined with high-lacquered redwood that made it look a little like a yacht deck.

The placard said the truck had originally been bought and modified by Charlie Bonner in 1951. Charlie had won eighteen straight races against his local high school friends before the nineteenth sent him crashing through a guard rail at Tequesta Canyon. Charlie had died, but his younger brother'd managed to salvage the car, and though he was now a busy architect, he still managed to drive it all over the South to place it in shows and displays.

Kurt didn't bother reading all this. With a swipe of his

hand he knocked the placard to the ground. "Get in!" he motioned to the other terrorist. The terrorist opened the driver's door and quickly dove into the truck. Kurt remained in the open door with Debbie pressed close to him. "Start it," he said.

The terrorist pulled some wires from beneath the dashboard, unwrapped the black electrical tape, and touched two wires together. They sparked and the truck started up with a roar. The terrorist, still keeping his head down, pressed the gas pedal with his hand to keep the motor going.

"Use the choke, asshole," Kurt said. He threw Debbie into the cab, practically on top of the other terrorist. He jumped in behind her, slammed the Chevy into gear, and squealed out of there, tires laying black rubbery trails across the glossy mall floor.

Just as the Chevy slowed to drive through the opening Hunter's truck had made through the entrance doors, Hunter leaped out from behind a concrete planter and grabbed the tailgate. But before he could pull himself into the bed, the hotrod truck lurched forward, knocking the rhythm of his running feet off. He kept a tight grip on the tailgate, but now he was being dragged by the truck, dragged across the broken glass from the shattered doors. A long sliver sliced into his shin. Still he held on.

But not for long.

The Chevy tore around the corner of the parking lot, hit an enormous speed bump, and shook his grip loose. Hunter was flung into a parked yellow Datsun, his elbow breaking the driver's window.

"Damn!" he muttered, climbing to his feet. He unslung the SMG from his back and took aim at the truck, but it was already pulling into traffic.

The loud obnoxious horn of John Eagle's pickup blared out the first four notes of "How the West Was Won" as Dahlia McGuire burst out of the mall, swerving to avoid a family of new shoppers just arriving. She hit the horn and the same four notes played. She pulled up to Hunter.

"That's the weirdest horn I ever heard," she said.

"He was a music lover," Hunter said, pulling open her door and shoving her aside. He stomped the gas and the truck sped off after Kurt.

Traffic was heavy due to the Christmas shopping, but not as heavy as in the past. The riots and random acts of violence had kept a lot of people home.

"You're losing them," Dahlia said. She pointed at the alley the Chevy had just turned into.

"He's got headers," Hunter explained.

"So what? You've got headlights, too."

"Headers. They allow more exhaust to escape, thereby sucking gas faster into the engine. That means they can go real fast."

"Then step on the gas."

Hunter looked over at Dahlia. Her face was grimly determined as she strapped on the safety belt. He smiled. "You got it, lady." He stomped the gas pedal to the floorboard and the truck swung around the corner and down the alley like a runaway train.

Dahlia pressed her back into the seat, holding onto the dashboard out of fear. Her lips were taut over gritted teeth. "My ex-husband used to drive like this."

"Yeah? He chase a lot of terrorists?"

"If they wore pantyhose he would have."

Hunter saw the Chevy up ahead. Kurt could drive fast, but he didn't drive well. He was losing a lot of time on the corners because he kept braking through them instead of

139

gassing through. Within minutes, Hunter's pickup was only eight feet behind Kurt. He could see Debbie struggling between the two men.

"Now what?" Dahlia asked. "We shoot out their tires?"

"That might sent them crashing."

"Right. We don't want to hurt Debbie."

Hunter felt a chill at the base of his skull. Until that moment he hadn't really thought about Debbie's safety at all. He didn't want the truck to crash because he wanted one of the terrorists alive so he could find out where Rostov was. He hadn't let them escape the mall because of Debbie. He'd been more concerned about the police arriving and arresting all of them, preventing him from tracking Rostov. Out here in the dark he could do what he wanted.

"You okay?" Dahlia asked.

"Fine. Get ready."

"For what?"

"This." Hunter swerved the pickup around to the passenger's side of the Chevy. The terrorist poked his Ingram submachine gun out the window and opened fire. The bullets pelted Hunter's windshield, smashing the safety glass into a pattern of cracked ice impossible to see out of. Hunter punched the glass in front of him, knocking out enough windshield to see. He dropped behind the Chevy again.

"Here." He handed Dahlia the H&K. "You know how to shoot?"

"I've done some trap shooting."

"Same principle. Come here."

She frowned at him. "Where? In your lap?"

"Here." He leaned forward, indicating the space between his back and seat.

"What'll I do?"

140

"Wait for the right moment. Then shoot the guy without hitting the driver."

"Or Debbie."

He kept his eyes straight ahead. "Of course."

Dahlia kicked off her flat shoes and climbed onto the seat. With great difficulty, she wedged herself behind Hunter. He leaned as far forward as he could and still drive.

"One of us needs to lose a few pounds," he said.

"Watch it, buster."

"Here goes." Hunter floored the pedal again, creeping up alongside the Chevy.

Again the terrorist leaned out the window and rattled off a burst of fire. Hunter yanked the wheel to the right, scraping a few parked cars. The bullets broke the overhead lights on top of the cab.

Hunter jerked the wheel to the left and his bigger pickup bumped the Chevy dragster, bouncing it off course. Kurt fought for control as the rear wheels wavered across the pavement.

Hunter stepped on the gas again. But this time when the terrorist leaned out the window, Hunter opened his own door, swung out so that one hand still gripped the steering wheel while the other held the door. He was suspended two feet above the racing pavement, his right foot still jammed against the gas pedal.

The terrorist leaned farther out the window for a better downward angle.

"Now, goddamn it!" Hunter yelled.

Dahlia aimed the SMG and squeezed the trigger, imagining the terrorist's face to be nothing more than a yellow-and-black clay pigeon her father had taught her to shoot. The bullets punctured his arm first, then walked up to his

141

shoulder, neck, and the side of his head. His body jerked at each bullet's impact, though he was dead before the last spray of bullets removed the top of his head.

Debbie screamed and screamed.

"Shut up!" Kurt hollered and struck her with the back of his hand.

"For God's sake, Hunter," Dahlia said, "get back up here."

Still hanging half out of the pickup, Hunter steered closer to the Chevy and reached for the handle to the passenger's door. Blood from the dead terrorist slumped over the window dripped down on his hand. With a quick yank, Hunter pulled open the door. The dead man spilled out of the Chevy onto the road. The back tires of both the Chevy and Hunter's pickup ran over the body.

"Grab her!" Hunter said.

Dahlia looked through the open doors of both trucks and saw Debbie's sobbing face, blood and mucus leaking from her nose where Kurt had hit her. And then there was Kurt, his eyes wide and crazed as he steered with one hand and fumbled for his gun with the other. Dahlia wondered if she should try to shoot him rather than grab for Debbie. But Debbie was in the way.

"Grab her! Now!" Hunter yelled.

Dahlia tossed aside her SMG and reached across from one truck to the other. "Help me, Debbie."

Debbie immediately lunged for Dahlia. But Kurt, not knowing whether to go for the gun or the girl, decided on the girl, grabbing her by the back of the blouse. Part of it tore away but he still had a tight enough grip that she couldn't move.

Dahlia wrapped her hands around Debbie's wrists and

pulled. The blouse tore a little more and Debbie eased closer to Dahlia.

"I'd appreciate you hurrying," Hunter said. His arms were tiring.

Dahlia tugged harder. More blouse tore. Debbie surged forward.

Hunter swerved the truck into the Chevy again. The impact sent the Chevy skidding slightly, and Kurt had to release his grip on Debbie to regain control of the hotrod. Dahlia immediately pulled, and Debbie dove across the seat into Dahlia's arms.

But not before Kurt managed to snag one of Debbie's ankles, still holding her. He steered the car slightly away and Debbie screamed at the sudden tension on her joints. Hunter also steered to the left, keeping the trucks within inches of each other. Debbie was stretched between the two trucks.

"Can't you shoot him?" Dahlia said.

"I don't have any hands left," Hunter replied.

With her free foot, Debbie kicked at Kurt's hand, but her soft plastic shoes were more fashionable than practical. Kurt kept his grip firm and began pulling her back into the cab.

"Son of a bitch is strong," Dahlia said. She had her arms around Debbie's waist, her feet jammed against the side of the cab for leverage.

Suddenly Kurt jerked the Chevy to the right, banging the open door Hunter was hanging on to. The door crumpled slightly and Hunter almost lost his grip. He sagged farther out of the truck, his back almost scraping the pavement before he pulled himself up again.

Slowly Hunter steered the truck to the right. Debbie

hollered, but Hunter kept easing the truck a little more to the right.

"My leg," Debbie cried.

Kurt's grip, though firm, was almost hampered by the sweat on his palms and the sweat on Debbie's bare leg. As his slippery hand slid along her ankle, he could feel the tiny bristles where she'd missed shaving. His hand was bunched up against her thin anklet sock as the pink cotton began to slide over her ankle bones, over her heel. Her shoe began to come off too. Kurt tried to tighten his grip, but it was no use. The shoe and sock popped off and Debbie sprang into Hunter's truck like a rubber band.

Hunter saw Kurt reaching for his Ingram. Immediately he pulled himself up, his shoulder bumping Debbie the rest of the way inside, shoving her so hard against Dahlia that both of them grunted. Hunter pulled the door shut behind him, but the damage it had sustained prevented it from staying closed. He swerved the wheel once more, bumping the Chevy hard. While Kurt fought for control again, Hunter picked up his own weapon, stuck it out the window, and fired.

The Chevy shot forward with a burst of speed, then wavered erratically before smashing into a parked Toyota, flipping, and bursting into flames.

Hunter stopped the truck, jumped out, and ran over to the flaming Chevy. He could see Kurt, wounded, struggling to crawl out of the overturned pickup.

Hunter stood less than ten feet away.

"Help me," Kurt said.

"Rostov."

"For God's sake, help me, Hunter." The flames made the bloody gash on his forehead look even redder.

"Rostov."

Kurt looked over his shoulder at the flames starting to fill the cab. He began pulling himself through the open window.

"I don't think you've got the time, Kurt."

Kurt was halfway through the window when the fire caught his pants. "Help me!" he screamed, swatting at his useless legs.

Hunter walked away. "You okay?" he asked Debbie as he climbed into the cab.

Then the Chevy exploded one more time. There was a sound, maybe a scream. It was too short to tell. Debbie and Dahlia both stared at him with something like fear. Hunter put the truck in gear and drove off. He was used to those looks.

"No, nothing."

"Did you tell him the real reason for the explosion?"

"No, I told him that it was some noise, I didn't—"

13

Rostov's punch knocked Tomas backwards into the cement wall. "What did you tell him?"

"Nothing. I swear."

Rostov calmly dabbed at the blood on his knuckles with a white silk handkerchief. The blood was Tomas's. "You only prolong the agony."

"You're crazy! Hunter is dead. I couldn't tell a dead man anything."

Rostov smiled. He did not look up. He concentrated on a particularly stubborn spot of blood before realizing that it was indeed a cut on his own knuckle. He chuckled. "Why don't you people ever get your teeth fixed. Look what your overbite has done." He held up his hand. The cut was so slight as to be barely noticeable. "I suppose that means our bloods have mixed. That makes us almost blood brothers, eh, Tomas?"

Tomas nodded eagerly. "Sure, Rostov. Blood brothers."

"And blood brothers never lie to one another."

"I'm not lying."

"But you failed to show up at the shopping mall. Very inconsiderate."

"Okay, I fucked up. I was with some broad. I didn't think—"

Rostov punched Tomas in the stomach. Tomas dropped to his knees. Rostov turned to face Nikko, who was leaning against the far wall. A single 60-watt light bulb swung slightly in the middle of the room, constantly shifting shadows. They were in the basement of a safe house Nikko had rented months ago. "Hunter was there, wasn't he?"

"Hunter is dead! Tell him, Nikko."

Nikko didn't say anything. He just watched.

Rostov smiled. "Nikko did a little checking for me, Tomas. Seems you met someone earlier, someone with a grenade. The descriptions match Hunter perfectly. But how can this be, I wonder, if Hunter is dead? I did kill him, didn't I?"

Tomas started to answer, to say anything, any lie he could think of. But Rostov grabbed hold of his freshly bandaged hand, the one that Hunter had first shot and then pinned to the wall with a knife. Rostov held the hand loosely in his own, examining it.

"Looks like you've had a little bleeding again, Tomas," Rostov said. "I thought it had stopped bleeding."

"It's nothing," Tomas said.

"You are too modest, my blood brother." Rostov suddenly gripped the hand hard, grinding the bones of the knuckles, tearing open the fragile wound.

Tomas cried out and fell to his knees in pain. Tears spilled from his eyes, mixing with the blood on his face.

"I did kill Hunter, didn't I, Tomas?" Rostov squeezed again. "Didn't I?"

"Yes!" Tomas wailed again.

"But how can this be?" He turned to Nikko. "This is puzzling. Hunter was there at this shopping mall, yet Tomas was not. Nikko, what is the answer?"

Nikko smiled.

Still clutching the mangled hand, Rostov stooped over and leaned his face a couple of inches from Tomas's. Tomas reeled slightly as if he might faint. "Nikko says that the only answer is that you talked to Hunter. What did he say?"

Tomas lifted his eyes weakly.

Rostov used both hands now to crush Tomas's hand. Tomas fell over writhing in agony as Rostov squeezed and kicked at his head. Rostov was almost in a frenzy when he shouted again, "What did he say?"

"He said . . ." Tomas's words were barely audible. Rostov stopped squeezing and kicking to listen. Tomas lifted his head from the cement floor. His expression was beyond pain, beyond care. He knew now what his fate was, knew there was no way out. Even smeared with blood, barely able to focus, his eyes looked defiant. "He said . . . to tell you . . . 'It's time to die.' " Tomas grinned.

Rostov dropped Tomas's hand and stepped back. His face was contorted with a sudden blast of fear and hatred. He snatched the .45 automatic from his belt, pressed it against Tomas's grinning face, and fired four times.

"Mikal!" Nikko shouted, running over. He grabbed Rostov from behind, felt the crazed man's hot fear burning through his clothes. "Enough."

Rostov spun and faced Nikko. "I have to kill him. Hunter."

"We have no time. We cannot be distracted from our work here."

"It will be done. It must be done. Now."

"Be reasonable, my friend. We cannot afford to divert our comrades from their assignments just to find one lone man."

"Then I will do it myself."

"No, Mikal. You mustn't. Everyone else here is expendable. But you are what holds us all together. Without you to lead, we would be just a gang of disorganized, undisciplined petty criminals. Everything depends on you."

Rostov looked down at Tomas's corpse. There was no more head, just a raw flap of butchered meat hanging from the neck, something one might feed to a large dog. He kicked Tomas's ribs, stepped over the body, and started up the stairs. "Have someone clean up this mess."

14

"Is that the right chin, Debbie?" Lt. Green asked.

Debbie concentrated on the array of chins from the police Identikit, but finally just shook her head in frustration. "I don't know, Lieutenant. Can't I just go home now?"

"Soon, Debbie." This was the part Lt. Green hated most. Nagging the victims, keeping after them when all they wanted and needed was to go home to bed. To feel safe. Yeah, he understood the cop reasons why they had to keep her here, why it was important to get this done while it was still fresh in her mind, that by tomorrow she might not even remember what he looked like. Still, forcing her through all this made him feel a little like a criminal himself, a little dirty. "Try again, Debbie. Take your time."

She took a deep breath and nodded. "Okay. But I don't understand why you want him. He's the one who saved my life."

"We don't want to harm him, Debbie. We just want to talk with him. Understand?"

She shrugged. "I guess."

"Fine. You just keep working with Officer Barnes here and let us know when you've got something that looks like him. Then we can start on the woman."

"Have my parents gotten here yet?"

"They're on the way. I've got a squad car bringing them in right now. Okay?"

She seemed to relax. "Okay."

"Need anything else? Coffee?"

"I don't drink caffeine. I'd like some juice if you've got it."

"Well if we don't, we'll get some. I'll take care of it right now."

"Thanks."

He patted her shoulder and walked off to send one of the officers after some juice. One his way down the corridor, he saw Adams, the CIA honcho, sitting in an interrogation room with those FBI fuck-ups, Harmon and Leeds. Lt. Green walked into the room and shook his head. "This is some sight. The good, the bad, and the dumb. What's up, fellas?"

"We're just discussing the situation," Harmon said.

"Someone forget to invite me?"

"You were busy," Leeds said. Leeds sucked on an unlit pipe, jabbing the stem to make his point. He jabbed it to emphasize "busy."

Adams leaned back in his chair. Even in this dingy room in the company of these two drab agents, Adams looked snazzy and relaxed. In control. Lt. Green studied him again just as he always did whenever the two met. Whatever else he was, Adams was a pro, Lt. Green decided. And a damned good one. He gave the impression of cooperation, but never revealed anything. Under different circumstances, Lt. Green would have liked working with the man, but not right now. Not when he was the one being kept in the dark.

"Got an I.D. yet?" Adams asked.

"She's still picking out chins. And she's not too sure about the eyebrows."

"Keep us posted."

"I aim to please."

Leeds stabbed the air with his pipe. "I think our first priority should be to capture this vigilante."

Harmon nodded. "I agree. Get him off the streets as soon as possible."

Lt. Green laughed. "What about the terrorists? Think we ought to do something about them too?"

"Absolutely," Leeds said. "But we have to stop this self-styled Batman before too much is made of him. Otherwise every citizen will be out in the streets shooting anything that moves. We'll have total chaos."

"Christ, Leeds!" Lt. Green shouted. "We already got that. Look around. Half the cops phoned in sick. They're staying home to protect their families. Same thing with the firemen. Hell, it's the same everywhere, all over the country. Lots of people aren't leaving their homes. We got armed citizens in the streets from coast to coast. The cops, the feds, and the spooks together haven't been able to do one fucking thing to stop any of this yet. And when some poor son of a bitch finally does something right and saves a few lives, we go after him like he was some mad dog or something."

"We can't have people taking the law into their own hands," Harmon said.

"Ordinarily I would agree. But there's nothing ordinary about this situation. We're up against the wall, gentlemen. Let's just be grateful this guy and his woman know what they're doing."

Leeds sucked air through his pipe. "At least the National Guard has finally been called up. They should be hitting the streets any minute now."

"Yeah, that should help add more panic to the situation."

"What's your suggestion, Lt. Green?" Adams said. "We just arm the private citizens and let them shoot whomever they please?"

Lt. Green smiled as he walked over to Adams. "It might help if you leveled with us, Adams."

"What do you mean?"

"I mean you don't seem very curious about who this guy is or how he knew where to be. I mean why haven't you questioned Debbie yet, or even looked at the composite drawing?"

Harmon and Leeds looked at Adams.

Adams's smile was boyish and charming. "I'm not here to step on toes or meddle in your investigation. I'm here to help coordinate Agency efforts to track down these maniacs."

"Yeah, but you know a hell of a lot more than you're telling us. I think you even know who this so-called vigilante is. Don't you?"

Adams laughed. "Yeah, it's really me. Whoops, guess you discovered my secret identity. My crime-busting days are over now, folks."

Harmon and Leeds laughed with him.

Lt. Green nodded. "Fine. You've convinced Heckle and Jeckle here. Meantime, we've had four more bombings in Miami and Miami Beach. There's a full-scale riot over by Old Cutler Road and Sunset. And we don't have enough cops to do anything but go over and yell through bullhorns. Meantime, you three keep up the good work.''

Lt. Green marched out of the room in search of juice.

15

Hunter was naked except for the towel wrapped around his waist. Water dripped down onto his shoulders and chest from his still-wet hair. From there the drops got lost in the thick matting of blondish hair that covered his body. The towel was too small to stay up on its own, so Hunter had to hold it closed with one hand.

"Your clothes are still drying," Dahlia said, pointing her pen at the dryer down the hall. She sat at the kitchen table writing notes. She wore a white terrycloth robe. A towel was wrapped around her hair.

"Do you have a larger towel I could use in the meantime?"

"Sorry, they're all dirty." She smiled. "I don't get to the laundry too often."

Hunter looked around the apartment. It was a mess. Dirty coffee cups were everywhere, discarded clothing draped here and there. Open books and scattered newspapers made it look like a kennel. Grimy pots and pans were stacked in and around the sink.

Dahlia followed his gaze. "Hey, I'm a reporter not a housekeeper, okay?"

"Do you have another robe?"

She shook her head. "Just this one. I'd offer you a pair of my sweat pants, but if they fit you I'd feel compelled to start dieting, and I'm not in the mood."

Hunter walked over to her and plucked the towel from her hair.

"Hey!" she protested.

He wrapped it around his waist, tucked it into a knot, then let the smaller one fall. He folded it and laid it on the table.

"Don't try to impress me with how neat you are," she said. "I don't consider neatness a virtue."

"Apparently." He padded across the kitchen floor, leaving a trail of wet footprints, and opened the refrigerator.

"Help yourself," she said.

"Nice of you to offer." He reached in and grabbed a Tupperware container with the lid half off. He sniffed, made a sour face. "This thing deserves a decent burial."

"I don't cook."

"We're not talking cooking, we're talking wrapping. You're supposed to press the lid until it hisses all the air out."

"Well, well, another bit of information from the mystery man. Weapons expert, spy, adventurer, and now Tupperware King."

"I'm a man of many talents." He rooted through the refrigerator, sniffing everything as he took it out. Some stuff he threw into the garbage, some he stacked on the counter. "How about an omelet, Ms. McGuire?"

Dahlia threw down her pen and jumped to her feet. "I will not be made a fool of in my own goddamn home. You want food? Okay, I'll cook it. Anybody can make a goddamn omelet. You don't have to be a genius." She pushed him away from the stove, accidentally brushing his towel with her hip. The towel unknotted and dropped to the floor. They both bent down for it at the same time and knocked heads.

"Ow," she said, rubbing her forehead. She looked into his eyes and laughed. They both laughed. Then they stopped laughing and started kissing. They forgot about the towel.

They stood, pulling each other closer, their mouths suctioned together, tongues thrashing. She felt his hardness against her hip and hugged him even tighter.

She pulled away a moment. "You want me to carry you into the bedroom?"

He smiled. "I'll walk."

"Least you could do is show some enthusiasm and run."

They did.

The bedroom was an even bigger mess than the rest of the apartment. They had to tramp over a week's worth of discarded clothing to reach the bed, but once they did they fell into each other's arms with the comfortableness of people who'd been together many times before. The first time they made love they were fast and hungry. The second time they were slow and exploring, patient.

Afterwards they lay holding each other, drifting in and out of a light sleep.

"Hunter?"

"Yeah?"

"Tell me about your deep dark days as a spook. Unless it's classified."

159

"Not to me."

"Good. What did you do?"

"This and that. Mostly killed people. Sometimes with a gun, sometimes with a knife, mostly with my hands." He reached out and brushed her cheek with the back of his hand.

"Jesus, you really know how to put a girl in the mood."

"Either you got it or you don't. What about you, how'd you get to be Lois Lane?"

"Columbia University. Knocked around freelance awhile before landing this job. Married my photographer. He was the best photographer I'd ever seen."

"What happened?"

She shrugged. "The usual."

"What'd you do then?"

"Bought my own camera."

He laughed.

A long silence followed as each lay back and stared at the cheap flashing Christmas tree.

"Hunter?"

"Hmmm."

"Now what do we do?"

He sat up, kissed her on the shoulder.

She laughed. "That's not what I mean and you know it."

He knew, but he was silent.

She turned. The room was dark except for the tiny plastic tree on the dresser. Its colored lights blinked on and off, throwing a kaleidoscopic pattern across Dahlia's naked body. "What's going to happen with all these bombings and riots?"

"I don't know. There's not much the government can do against its own citizens except keep the violence to a minimum and hope to ride it out."

"That won't work."

"The only other choice is to find Rostov and kill him before things get any more out of hand. He'll keep up the pressure until this country splits right down the middle. Destroy from within—that's always been the terrorist's credo."

She ran her fingers over his broad chest. Hard muscles moved beneath the soft hair. "You saved a lot of lives tonight."

"It's not enough."

"It's a start."

"They'll be after me, you know."

She nodded.

"I'm going to need your help."

"As long as I get the exclusive."

He looked at her. The green and red lights reflected off her tan breasts like neon freckles. "It's nice to know you're not going to turn soft on me."

She smiled. "I won't if you won't."

16

The newsroom was nearly empty. Assistant Metro editor Davis Clayborne was yelling into the phone so loudly that even the clacking of word-processor keyboards couldn't drown him out.

"You don't have a fucking family, Osgood," he shouted. "And if you don't get your ass in here within thirty minutes, you won't have a fucking job either." He slammed the phone down and turned to face Dahlia.

"Still making friends the hard way, huh?" she said.

"Poor son of a bitch Osgood. Tells me he can't come in, has to stay home and protect his family. He's so scared he forgot I've been over to his cheesy apartment. I know his whole life story. He's got one cousin somewhere in Oregon and that's it."

Dahlia nodded at the empty desks around the newsroom. "What about the others?"

Clayborne shrugged his beefy shoulders. "They're not coming in, McGuire. The only ones here are those without

163

families like you and me, or those with a great sense of responsibility and duty like Dan Logan.''

"Can't we be part of both groups? Alone and responsible?"

Clayborne grinned, wiped some ink from his fingers onto his loud tie. "Nope. When it all starts falling apart, it's the lonely that try the hardest to put it back together. They're the ones who haven't gotten what they need yet."

"You're a real philosopher, Davis."

"You think?" He grinned even wider.

Dahlia walked over to Dan Logan's office and rapped on the door. She could see him staring at the small Sony TV on his bookshelf. His eyes looked sunken and suddenly old. When he didn't respond to her knock, she tried again.

He looked up and waved her in. "Take a seat, McGuire."

She did. Together they watched some of the newsclips from around the country. Rioting was coast to coast now, with few police to do anything about it. Fires raged, but response time was about two hours, if the firefighters even showed up. The stock market was a disaster; schools were closing everywhere; the National Guard was patrolling in every state, despite the large number of AWOL troops. The litany of disaster continued, but Dan Logan reached over and turned down the sound. He swiveled around and faced Dahlia.

"So, what's new?"

She laughed. "Nice to know you can keep your sense of humor."

"That's why I make the big bucks around here."

Dahlia looked into his haggard face. "Where're June and the kids?"

"Upstairs, the boss's office."

"You brought them here?"

"Why not? It's obvious that the terrorists aren't going to harm any of the media works as long as we continue to publicize their destruction. So this is probably the safest place for them."

Dahlia nodded. "Pretty smart. But then, that's why you make the big bucks."

"What are you working on now?"

"Davis wants me to check out the results of all this on the food supply. Follow it from the growers to the supermarket to the people, that kind of thing."

"What about your mystery caller? Anything more from him?"

"Not since yesterday. I dropped a copy of the tape off at the cop shop, asked them if they wanted to set up their tracing equipment and stuff."

"What'd they say?"

"They don't have the manpower. Asked me to call them if he phones again."

"They're probably right. Whoever this guy is, he knows better than to let himself get traced. That's a dead end." He rooted through the papers on his desk, found the composite drawings of Hunter and Dahlia and slid them across the desk. "You know anything about what happened at the mall last night?"

Dahlia stared at Dan, searching his face. No, he didn't know. She looked at the sketches; they weren't recognizable. "I'm working on an angle right now that includes the mall."

"What kind of angle?"

"I can't talk about it yet."

"Come on, McGuire. Give me something."

"Something to do with the vigilante."

Dan Logan sat straight up, excited, his old news instincts taking over again. "What do you know?"

"I've got a lead, a source. I think it's going to give us a hell of an exclusive."

He looked at her carefully, nodding. Then he glanced down at the sketch.

Now he knows, Dahlia realized.

"Want to run it by legal first?" he asked. "I think one of the attorneys showed up today."

"Don't worry, everything's under control."

"Be careful, okay?"

"I will. Let me pop up and say hi to June. Any message?"

"Tell her I'll be up in a couple of hours with lunch."

Dahlia returned to her desk first, sorting out some of the messages. The dentist had cancelled her appointment indefinitely. A guy from the mayor's office she had a date with was also cancelling; he was leaving town. Nothing else that couldn't wait.

The phone rang.

The buzz startled her and she almost snatched it right up. But then she remembered her training and attached the suction-cup microphone and punched the Record button. "McGuire."

"Ah, Ms. McGuire. Still coming to work, eh? We chose well."

"Get on with it."

"Is that any way to treat an informant? What if you angered me and I hung up?"

"Don't try to con me, buster. You're using this paper and every other news outlet as your personal publicity service. So just give me the details of the next big caper and I'll be there."

The voice laughed. "You are an interesting woman, Ms. McGuire. I hope we can meet face-to-face someday."

The tone of his voice made Dahlia's stomach clench. "Sure, let's have lunch real soon."

He laughed again. "When this is all over, I shall make a point of seeing you. But in the meantime, I think your paper will profit by going down to Okeechobe Road and Seventy-fourth Street."

"Why? What's happening?"

"Nothing yet. But soon. A fresh army will be swarming through your streets. And then it will truly be American against American."

"What are you talking about? Where exactly do you want me to go?"

He hung up.

"Damn!" Quickly she dialed her home number.

"Yeah?" Hunter answered.

"He just called." She repeated the conversation from her notes. "What do you think?"

"I don't know. What's over there?"

"Not much. The Miami International Airport is nearby, over on Dolphin Expressway. The Opa Locka Airport is northeast of there. Hialeah Racetrack. I don't know what else. It doesn't make any sense."

"He said, 'American against American,' right?"

"Yeah, but that's already been going on."

"True, but mostly along racial lines. I think he's talking about something less obvious." There was a long silence on the phone. "Any prisons over there?"

"Jesus, Matt."

"Come on, McGuire, there isn't much time. What's over there?"

"The new Coral Prison facility. Holds twelve hundred

and fifty convicts, a lot of them hard-core criminals. There was a hell of a fight about constructing the thing within the city.''

''That would be the next logical step. Once the jails and prisons are emptied, we won't know who to trust. People will shoot at anything that moves.''

''I'll meet you,'' she said.

''No! Stay there. This isn't going to be a photo opportunity, it's going to be a battlefield.''

''Oh, not like last night, huh?''

Hunter hesitated. ''That was different.''

''Look, Hunter. Just because we slept together, don't get all protective. I'm still a reporter.'' She sighed, softened her voice. ''I appreciate the thought though. Really. It's just that I can't sit around and be afraid. I've got to do something. Just like you. Understand?''

''I understand. Be careful.''

''You too. Listen, the place is crawling with National Guard. And thanks to your well-publicized antics last night, a whole new crop of vigilantes has taken to the streets. You won't have a lot of friends out there.''

Hunter's laugh was harsh. ''Just like always.''

''Not quite,'' Dahlia said. ''I'll be out there.''

17

Traffic was sparse but confusing. Another bomb had knocked out some of the city's traffic lights, others were flashing red. Horns honked impatiently, and drivers hurled insults and curses at each other.

Hunter was one of those waiting in line at a flashing red light. The VW bug two cars ahead was stalled. Suddenly the driver in the car in front of Hunter jumped out, ran to the VW, and yanked the teenage driver out.

"It's stalled, mister," the boy pleaded.

"Then push it the fuck out of the way." The burly man shoved the kid into the car.

A young girl, about eighteen, climbed out of the passenger's side of the bug. "It's flooded. Just give it a minute and we'll be out of here."

"I don't got a minute, girlie."

"Then pull around us."

"Don't go telling me what to do." He grabbed the

skinny boy by the shirtfront and raised a fist. "How'd you like me to pound your boyfriend into dog shit?"

Hunter honked his horn.

The burly man looked back.

Hunter smiled, crooked a finger at the man.

"What the fuck's your problem, asshole?" the man shouted.

Hunter waved the man toward him.

Uncertain, the man pushed the kid away and swaggered toward Hunter's pickup. When he was halfway there, Hunter tapped the gas pedal and let the truck smack into the man's tan Nova.

"Jesus!" the man said. Now he was really mad, charging toward Hunter like a rampaging bull. "Gonna kick your ass into next week, asshole!"

Hunter waited until the man was almost to the cab, then abruptly swung the door open, slamming it into his face and chest. The man dropped to the ground, groaning. The two kids jumped back into their bug, started the engine, and sped through the intersection. Hunter pulled around the Nova, waited his turn, and drove on.

The people on the streets walked with wary suspicion, eyeing everyone they saw. Some carried weapons openly, a knife, an axe, a baseball bat. Others wore long coats to conceal their weapons.

The sun was bright and hot with Christmas only a few days away. No one was carrying gifts anymore.

Hunter kept to the back streets and the alleys. The cops here would be too few and too busy to worry about him.

He turned down Mango Street and found the road blocked by piles of debris, old mattresses, furniture, rusty bikes, an overturned police car.

Six men stood behind the barricade, each with a white rag torn from a sheet tied around his upper arm. Each man carried a weapon, though only two had guns, both rifles. One man had a spear gun.

"Now what?" Hunter mumbled, inching the truck slowly toward the barricade. This street was the fastest, safest way to where he was going.

"What's your business, man?" one of the men called. He carried one of the rifles.

"Looking for a way home, that's all."

"Go another way!"

"This way's faster."

The man opened fire with his rifle, shooting through the space where the windshield once was. The bullet thumped into the passenger seat. The man stopped shooting and hollered again, "This way's deader."

Hunter waved and slowly turned the pickup around. He heard the men cheer each other, one of them laughing, saying, "He'll think twice before he fucks with this neighborhood."

Hunter was about thirty feet from the barricade when he jerked hard on the wheel and stomped the gas pedal, sliding the pickup around so it faced the barricade again. His foot mashed the pedal and the truck blasted straight for the barricade.

The vigilantes raised their weapons and fired, but they were too shaken to be accurate. A spear zipped through the open windshield and burried itself in the seat a few inches from Hunter's arm.

When the truck hit the barricade, debris and men alike scattered. The man with the spear gun lay on the ground, dazed by a blow from a flying bicycle wheel. Hunter braked next to him, plucked the spear from his seat, and tossed it on the ground next to the man. "You may need this," he said and sped away. No gunfire followed him.

Hunter was close to the area Rostov had told Dahlia about. The Coral Prison was only another mile away. He stepped on the gas and raced through a deserted intersection, ignoring the flashing red light.

A National Guard jeep suddenly shot out of an alley and swung in behind him. There were two men in the jeep. The passenger raised his bullhorn. "Pull over to the side," he commanded.

Hunter looked in the rearview mirror. The driver was already on the radio.

"Pull over," the bullhorn said again. "Pull over or we will open fire."

Hunter saw the second jeep now, coming straight ahead. He pulled the pickup over to the side of the road and slid his H&K SMG closer. Through the rearview and side mirrors he watched the two men climb out of their jeep. The passenger walked toward Hunter's window, unsnapping his holster. The driver, clutching an M-16, took up a post behind the pickup.

The two men in the second jeep also got out and started toward the pickup. Both carried M-16s. One of them, the shorter one, wore mirrored sunglasses and fingered his gun anxiously.

The guardsman from the first jeep reached Hunter first. "Got any I.D., sir?" The "sir" sounded like "asshole."

"Sure, son. Have some right here somewhere." Hunter reached over toward the glove compartment. "Let me get my wallet."

The two approaching guardsmen were almost at the pickup. The shorter one removed his sunglasses. It was Koyo. He nodded at the guardsman next to Hunter. The guardsman nodded back and smiled. Slowly he removed his pistol from his holster and aimed it at Hunter's back.

"Here it is," Hunter said. He twisted around and squeezed off a burst from the SMG. The guardsman's chest opened up as he flew backwards into the street.

Koyo and the other two terrorists opened fire on the cab just as Hunter kicked open the passenger's door and rolled out onto the sidewalk. He came up shooting, killing the dead guardsman's companion. That left Koyo and his partner.

Hunter dropped flat to the ground, wedging himself in the gutter between the pickup and the curb. He watched Koyo's feet sneaking along one side of the cab while the second man's feet slowly crept toward the other side.

When Koyo's feet stepped over the dead guardsman, they paused. It was as if he suddenly knew where Hunter was. Hunter sensed it, too, for he immediately opened fire on the feet, the bullets shredding the shins and ankles of both legs. Koyo collapsed to the ground screaming. Another blast from Hunter sent Koyo's gun skidding out of reach.

"Koyo!" the last man yelled. But before Hunter could open up on his feet, too, the man hopped up onto the hood of the truck. The pickup bounced from his weight. Hunter heard the man denting metal with each step as he crawled over the truck.

Hunter rolled under the pickup and began scooting toward the front of the truck. He would have to be careful this time; he needed a couple of live ones to question.

"Koyo, where is he?" the terrorist asked, but Koyo's pain kept him writhing, barely conscious. Blood pooled around his useless feet.

Hunter pulled himself out from under the pickup and

quietly kneeled, waiting. He heard the terrorist climb down to the bed of the truck, walk around looking for a target, then climb back up to the top of the cab for a better look. "The bastard has run," he said in Polish.

That's when Hunter sprang out from behind the fender, whacked the man's shins with his SMG, and watched him fall face first onto the hood of the truck. Immediately Hunter bounced the man's head off the hood and dragged him from the truck, flinging him onto the ground next to Koyo.

"Can we talk?" Hunter said.

Koyo pulled himself up to a sitting position. "Go fuck yourself, Hunter," he said in Japanese.

"Too bad," Hunter answered in Japanese. He fired a short burst into Koyo's chest, killing him instantly.

"How about you?" Hunter asked in Polish.

"Okay, okay. Don't shoot." The man spoke in a Krakow dialect.

"Where's Rostov? The prison?"

"You know about that?"

"Is he there?"

"No. That was Koyo's job. Rostov is leading another mission."

Hunter aimed the SMG at the terrorist's face. "I'm listening."

18

"Are we going to die, Daddy?" Sally asked her father.

"No, baby." Daryl Hagen took his six-year-old daughter's hand in his and guided her across the street. Next to him, his wife Lisa hurried with their infant son bundled in her arms.

"I feel funny about this," Lisa said. St. Anne's Catholic church loomed in front of them. She hesitated. "We aren't even Catholic."

"We aren't even anything," Daryl said. "But we're parents and this place is a hell of a lot safer than our home. Besides, you always wanted to study religion when we were in college."

"That's because I needed three more philosophy units to graduate, remember? I took logic instead."

"Well, now's the time to be logical. Let's go." He lifted Sally into his arms, kissed his wife on the cheek, and together they walked into the church.

The pews were almost filled with families of all colors

and races. They all turned nervously to stare at the new-comers. An audible sigh of relief sounded as they saw Daryl's family and relaxed.

The priest at the head of the congregation looked to be Daryl's age, barely thirty. He waved them in. "Come in, come in. It's all right. There are a lot of new faces here today. We don't care what your belief is or isn't. You are welcome. Some of you are here for shelter. Some for prayer. Those who do not wish to pray need not feel compelled to do so. Pray only if you wish. Then again"—he smiled out at them—"it couldn't hurt."

Daryl looked at Lisa and they both laughed. Many in the congregation also laughed.

"That is the sound that pleases God even more than prayer," the priest said.

"Daryl?" Lisa said.

"Yes?"

"I feel better." She reached over and squeezed his hand.

Outside the church, Rostov finished directing the placement of the last explosive charge.

"What about the school?" he asked Leif, the Swedish terrorist.

"They are still holding classes. The nuns are teaching them right now."

"Are the charges all set?"

"*Ja.* Everything is connected to the charge box across the street. Once the switch is flipped this church and the school next door will both be destroyed. I estimate a ninety-three percent kill factor." Leif had been an engineer at one time and considered himself better educated than the rabble he worked with. He never missed an opportunity to remind Rostov of that fact.

"Then let's get on with it." Rostov waved the three terrorists away from the buildings.

Nikko stepped out of the van across the street and faced Rostov.

"Come to watch the fun, Nikko?"

Nikko took Rostov's arm and pulled him away from the others. "I just spoke to one of our patrols. Hunter has killed Koyo and the others."

"And Hunter?"

Nikko shrugged. "Disappeared."

"The prison?"

"It is still intact."

Rostov's face hardened. He tugged at his sleeve, rubbing his scarred wrist. "Send someone else. Find Hunter."

"Mikal, there is no one else."

Rostov's eyes bulged angrily, though his voice was soft, almost a whisper. "I'll do it myself." He turned to Leif. "Finish this."

"Yes, sir." Leif saluted enthusiastically.

Rostov stalked off to his jeep, jumped in, and started it up. Nikko cursed under his breath and ran after him, hopping into the jeep just as it squealed away from the curb.

"I'm in charge now," Leif informed the other three terrorists. One of them rolled his eyes and mumbled under his breath. "Start unspooling the wire. Let's get some distance."

Two of them grabbed the large wooden spool and began backing away from the church into the parking lot. Leif waved his hand, directing them between the parked cars next to the rectory garage. The remaining terrorist held his gun ready and looked for police.

From inside the church they could hear the congregation singing "Ave Maria."

Leif lifted his hand, paused to relish the moment of glory, then sliced his arm downwards as if signaling the start of a race. "Now!"

One of the terrorists turned the switch on the black box, completing the circuit.

Nothing happened.

The Swede cursed and knocked the man at the box aside. "Fool! What have you done?" He fiddled with the wires, then twisted the switch again. Still nothing.

"Got a problem?" Hunter stood on the roof of the garage, holding a fist-sized hunk of plastic explosive with the charge still attached. He tossed it down at their feet. "This belong to any of you?"

The four men jumped out of the way, Leif tripping over two of them in his effort to escape the explosion. But again, nothing happened. The plastique lay in a ball at their feet, the charge sticking out, the wire running back up to the roof where Hunter stood.

"I pulled the charges from the other ones, but this one was too stubborn. I had to cut the wires." He kneeled on the roof and picked up the two ends of the severed wires. "See?"

Leif and his comrades climbed to their feet, all reaching for their guns. "Kill him!" Leif commanded.

"Gee, fellas, don't be sore," Hunter said. "I think I can still fix it." He touched the ends of the wires together and the plastique exploded immediately. Hunter flattened himself against the roof and felt the shower of blacktop, wood, plastic, and body parts on his back. Smoke swirled around him. When it settled, he peered over the edge of the roof, identified three gooey clumps that once might have been bodies, and saw Leif limping away.

Hunter vaulted off the edge of the roof. He landed in a tuck and roll, kipping to his feet right next to Leif. A spinning back kick knocked Leif into an orange Renault. The Swedish terrorist threw a left hook and a right cross, but Hunter blocked both, retaliating by grabbing a handful of blond hair and slamming the man's head backwards into the roof of the Renault, denting it.

"Just be glad it wasn't a Volvo," Hunter said. "Harder metal."

Leif sagged to the ground, unconscious.

19

Dahlia pulled her jeep into the parking lot of the Food Basket supermarket. The lot was full of cars. People were racing back and forth, their grocery carts overflowing with goods. Two aproned stockboys stood at the entrance to the store, each holding a shotgun and looking nervous.

Dahlia parked and approached the market cautiously. All she wanted was to use one of the pay phones near the entrance; but when she arrived, she saw that both of them had been jimmied and smashed.

She walked up to one of the stockboys, a sandy-haired kid no more than nineteen.

"You have another pay phone inside?" she asked.

"Yeah, in the deli section."

"Great." She started to enter.

"We may have to search you when you come back out. Shoplifting."

Dahlia glared at him with an icy smile. "You're welcome to try."

The other stockboy, lanky and dark haired, snorted. "Go on in, lady. I think we can trust you."

"Thanks," Dahlia said, entering. It was a bad sign when the kids that age started calling you "lady." She was barely thirty and already they were addressing her as if she were one of their mothers' friends.

The scene inside the supermarket put Dahlia in mind of the stock market on the day of the Big Crash. People were shoveling cans into their carts as fast as they could. Some people tried to push two carts, or had their child push an extra cart. Some were taking food out of other carts, throwing them into their own, and scooting away. Dahlia had to elbow her way past the crowds of carts bumping into each other, the fights over canned fruit. At the far corner she saw the deli sign.

The loudspeaker crackled, followed by an apologetic voice: *"Once again, ladies and gentlemen, I have to inform you that the situation on the streets has prevented any shipments of fresh produce or meat again today."*

A roar of protest rose from the crowd of shoppers. Dahlia continued struggling through. She passed the manager, who stood behind one of the closed checkstands speaking into the microphone. He was sweating profusely and kept fingering the pistol stuck in his belt.

"Attention, please," he continued, the shakiness in his voice amplified throughout the store. *"In an effort to insure fair distribution of our remaining stock, we must limit your purchases to twelve items. And only cash will be accepted."*

The cries of anger were even louder this time. A couple of people made a break for the door with their shopping carts, but the armed stockers stopped them. One man tried to push through anyway, and one of the stockers clipped him in the jaw with the gunstock.

Dahlia finally found the phone, thumbed in a quarter, and punched the numbers. "Hi, Dee Dee, it's Dahlia. Gimme Logan."

Pause.

"Logan here."

"Hi, Dan. You wouldn't believe it out here. I'm in a supermarket right now. The people are ready to kill each other over the food, and the prices are outrageous. Get this, a can of Heinz Vegetarian Baked Beans is two and a half bucks."

"Is that bad?"

"Jesus, Dan, you've got to get out more."

"What happened with the prison break?"

"Nothing. I waited on a nearby rooftop with my trusty camera, but nothing ever happened. Maybe after I tipped off the cops, the terrorists saw the extra guardsmen they sent over and decided to try later. I don't know."

"Anything from that vigilante?"

She felt a hot rush of worry in her stomach. "Haven't heard anything."

The phone was silent.

"Maybe you should come back in," Dan said. "I think it's getting kind of dangerous out there."

"Okay. I'll take a few shots of the market here so the trip won't have been a complete waste. I can write a feature by deadline."

"Fine. Hey, while you're there, pick up some eggs and cheese for me, okay?" He chuckled.

"In your ear," she said and hung up.

Dahlia snapped the flash attachment to her camera and clicked off a few shots of the shoppers fighting, ramming each others' carts. The grocery clerks were putting cans back on the shelves from people who had taken more than their alloted twelve items. Dahlia felt sorry for the shoppers. She understood their panic as they fought to feed themselves and their families. Her own cabinets were well-stocked with canned fruits and vegetables and boxes of pasta. Her parents visited every three months and felt compelled to fill the apartment with food, even though Dahlia kept explaining that she ate out almost all the time.

Dahlia exited through the electric eye. The two stockboys looked her over.

"Well?" she said, lifting her arms.

"That's okay," the sandy-haired kid said, waving her on.

She walked across the parking lot. A couple of National Guardsmen stood next to her jeep. One was talking on the car radio.

"What's the problem, men?" she asked, snapping their picture.

"Nothing, ma'am," one of them said. He was pale with a slight accent, maybe Slavic. His partner was dark-skinned, Latin-looking.

"Am I free to go?"

The pale one shrugged. "Certainly."

Dahlia climbed into her jeep and felt it tilt slightly to the left. She leaned out and looked at the front tire. It was flat. She looked back at the two men. They were trying not to grin.

Without saying a word, Dahlia hauled the jack out and unfastened the spare tire. The two guardsmen watched as she positioned the jack and pumped the side of the jeep up. They didn't offer to help.

The Latin driver nudged his partner and pointed. Another jeep with four more guardsmen was coming toward them. They exchanged waves and the jeep pulled into the parking lot and headed toward them.

Dahlia looked up, noticed the approaching jeep. The man in the passenger's side wore captain's bars.

He's going to get a piece of my mind, Dahlia thought, standing to meet him.

Hunter spoke into the phone. "Dahlia McGuire, please."

"I'll transfer," the woman said.

A brief pause.

"Dan Logan here," a man's gruff voice said.

"Is Dahlia McGuire there?" Hunter asked.

"No. I'm taking her calls while she's out. Any message?" Hunter thought it over. "No. Where can I reach her?"

"You can't. Which are you, the terrorist or the vigilante?"

"A friend."

Logan sighed. "Aren't we all?"

"Has her informant called again?"

"Ah, so you are the vigilante. Listen, she's out on a limb because of you. Don't saw it off."

"Where is she?"

Dan Logan told him. "She's covering a story, so don't—"

But Hunter had already hung up.

The jeep with the four guardsmen rolled across the parking lot, not halting as people with grocery carts or shopping bags scurried to their cars. Shoppers dodged out of the way.

The man in the captain's uniform stared straight ahead. Behind him, two more guardsmen manned a 7.62mm M60 machine gun on an M2 mount. One of the men had the butt stock pressed to his shoulder and his finger around the trigger. The other man was pushing a link of bullets into the feed-plate groove, waiting for the feed-plate retaining pawl to catch.

The man in the captain's uniform spoke to them in Russian. "Wait for my signal."

"Yes, Nikko," the men answered.

Nikko took deep breaths, controlled his anger. Rostov had stalked away from the job at the church and now word had come back that the church was still standing but their squad was dead. All because Rostov had rushed off like a child, obsessed with Hunter. Had they waited, Hunter would have come to them. Now Rostov was off cruising the streets looking for Hunter, while Nikko was forced to handle the operations himself. Rostov was too important for anything to happen to him right now. He had Moscow's faith and he had the men's fear. But when this was over, Nikko would arrange a little accident for his commander. Rostov had foolishly risked the mission and Nikko's life for the last time.

Nikko looked Dahlia McGuire over as they drove closer. A little thin, perhaps, but strikingly attractive. Her beauty was not so much in her features as in her stance, her attitude. She stared back at him with confidence, defiance. Nikko smiled. It would be amusing to watch her beg.

His men had been looking for her jeep or Hunter's truck all day. It had become clear from the accounts of a woman with Hunter at the mall last night and Hunter's presence in this area after Rostov's call to McGuire, that she somehow knew Hunter. With her in hand, perhaps they could force Hunter out of hiding. Nikko doubted it, though. Hunter was too much the professional for that. Still, maybe if they left one of her hands or feet on the seat of her jeep, it might inspire Hunter to come out.

"You in charge here?" Dahlia asked as the guardsmen braked next to her jeep.

"I am," Nikko said.

"Then maybe you can ask your little toy soldiers why they slashed my tire?"

Nikko turned to the two men in the first jeep. "Did you men slash this woman's tire?"

"Yes," the pale one answered.

Nikko smiled. "There you have it, Ms. McGuire."

Dahlia felt the fear clawing at her throat. Something wasn't right here. "You know me?"

"Everyone knows you. You are a famous journalist. Even my good friend Matt Hunter knows you, doesn't he?"

Dahlia tried to run, but Nikko caught her roughly by the arm, spun her around, and slapped her across the face. She cried out.

The two stockboys heard her cries and started running toward her, both cocking their shotguns.

Nikko snapped his fingers at the two Russians manning the M60. They swung it around and opened fire. The two stockboys stumbled and sprawled across the pavement, dead.

"Keep the others busy," Nikko said calmly.

The men opened fire on the shoppers as they hurried to their cars. Screams and cries chorused with the clacking machine gun as people were torn apart by the huge 7.62mm slugs. Another burst shattered the plate-glass window of the storefront.

Dahlia twisted and struggled in Nikko's grip. He laughed and slapped her again. Blood seeped from the corner of her mouth. "Tell us where Hunter is and we'll stop."

"I don't know any Hunter," she said.

He smacked her twice more, forehand and backhand. His knuckles left four round welts on her cheek. "Where is he?"

Suddenly the sound of the machine gun was interrupted by the lighter sound of another gun. And the roar of an engine.

Nikko looked up. Hunter's pickup was hurtling straight at them, his SMG poking out of the missing windshield, shaking and blazing as bullets thwacked into the jeep next to Nikko. The two men at the machine gun yelled and were blown out of the vehicle. The pale Slav shouldered his M-16 just as three bullets from Hunter's SMG tore open his throat.

Nikko locked an arm around Dahlia's neck and pulled her away. His other hand drew his .45 from its holster.

The driver of the first jeep tried to start the engine, but Hunter plowed into the vehicle, bouncing him out of the driver's seat and through the windshield of a Dodge Dart. Hunter's pickup spun around, banged into two parked cars, and flipped over on its side.

Nikko fired four shots through the bottom of the truck into what he thought was the floor of the cab. There was no movement from the truck. Still dragging Dahlia with him, Nikko cautiously approached.

"Come on, Hunter," he said. "Come out or I'll kill her."

No response.

Nikko slowly walked toward the cab. The driver's side was facing up. He looked around through the open windshield, but saw nothing. Carefully he peeked over the edge of the driver's closed window.

Empty.

"Hey, Nikko."

Nikko spun around just as Hunter popped up from between two parked cars. Hunter fired two shots, both of
which punched through Nikko's face, tearing off the back
of his head like a bird's nest. Blood and gunk splattered
Dahlia.

Hunter limped toward them, his gun still aimed at Nikko.
Hunter's clothes were ragged from his jump out of the truck.
Long skid marks on his thighs bled through his torn pants.

Dahlia ran to him, throwing her arms around his neck.
She kissed him hard on the lips. Her voice was soft and
grateful. "That's for saving my life."

"Anytime."

"And this is for risking it," she snapped, swinging a
fist at him. He blocked it and she swung again. He blocked
that too.

"What's the matter?"

"You could've killed me, you stupid bastard. He was
using me as a shield." She swung still again, and again
was blocked.

Hunter limped over to Nikko's jeep and climbed in.
"Guess I'd better leave before you get mad."

She looked around, found a spilled bag of groceries
from a runaway cart whose owner had been shot by Nikko's
men. She reached into the bag and threw a can of tomatoes
at him. It flew by, barely missing his head. She threw a
can of Spanish rice. It clunked off the hood. She threw a
can of Budweiser beer. Hunter caught it as he started up
the engine, popped the top, and sipped.

"Thanks," he said, lifting the can to her. He drove off.

No one came over to question or help her. Most continued to shop.

Dahlia changed the tire of her jeep and drove back to the
paper.

20

Adams sat in his Datsun 300Z and tapped out a tune from Madonna's new album. He was too old to like her, he thought, but somehow he did. As a kid playing Bob Dylan and Beatles records despite his parents' criticism, he'd made a pact that he would never outgrow rock 'n' roll. He knew the minute he stopped liking it, he'd have become his parents. It was like *Invasion of the Body Snatchers*; you fall asleep and you become one of Them.

Maybe it was already too late. You don't work for the CIA for all these years and still sing "White Rabbit" with the Jefferson Airplane.

Adams tapped out his tunes while studying his rearview mirror and glancing out all the windows. The parking lot of Miami International was almost empty after the bombing last night. Most flights had been suspended.

There was a loud metallic knocking on his roof and Adams jumped in his seat, his hand automatically diving for his gun. An upside-down face peered through his windshield. Hunter was smiling.

"Goddamn it," Adams said.

Hunter hopped down from the roof of the small car and climbed in the passenger's seat.

"Where'd you learn to do that?" Adams asked.

"Here and there."

"Bullshit. Some kind of *ninja* school or something, that's what I think. You lived in Japan as a kid, didn't you?"

"Can we get down to it?"

Adams watched a lone plane circling the airport. "I've been following your exploits. It would make a good TV show."

"Not until we have an ending."

"There is no ending on TV. Everything just goes on and on until it gets cancelled." He twisted around in his seat and pulled off his red-tinted glasses. "You've eliminated Koyo and Nikko, but Rostov is still out there directing traffic."

"I'm getting closer."

"Not fast enough. The cops and the FBI are hot on your ass, Hunter. Because of you, vigilantes are operating all over the country. Trouble is, sometimes they hit the wrong people."

"You brought me into this; you knew my methods."

"I also know that Lt. Green and the two FBI yokels around here are pulling out all the stops. They're determined to nail your butt to the barn door so all may see the error of your ways. And there's nothing I can do about it. We're not even supposed to know each other."

"How close are they?"

"They're raking their informants over the coals. They

even hauled in that woman reporter, McGuire. Witnesses caught her license number when you wiped out Nikko and his bunch at the supermarket. Will she talk?''

Hunter shrugged. ''She's her own person. But that's not the problem right now. Rostov is. The man's certifiable. Grade-A nuts. Nikko was the only thing keeping him in line. And now that Nikko is gone, there's nothing between him and pure carnage.''

''Except you,'' Adams said.

''Yeah, right. Only I can't find the bastard. Meantime, all the cops in the city are looking for me. And my old spook buddy in the fancy threads can't do anything about it.''

Adams smiled. ''Just like the old days, huh?''

''Yeah, that's why I got out.''

''That's not what I heard.''

''What did you hear?''

''A lot of conflicting stories. One goes that you were told to sanction a woman you loved. Another says you killed some senator's son who was selling his father's secrets to the Soviets. Another—''

''What do you believe?''

Adams grinned. ''All of them.''

Hunter laughed as he got out of the car.

''Hey, where are you going?''

''It's time to finish this thing.''

''How you going to find Rostov?''

''I've got my own sources, someone who knows the area well.''

''Watch yourself. Don't trust anybody.''

''Hell, Adams, I don't even trust you.''

''Me neither.'' Adams started up the car, waved, and sped away.

Hunter drove to the phone booth in the closest terminal. He fished for a quarter, dropped it into the slot. She answered on the first ring. "Home kind of early, aren't you?"

"My usual shift," Dahlia said. "I don't live at the paper, you know."

"You still mad?"

"I haven't decided."

"How about some fence-mending?"

Dahlia paused. "I'm listening."

Hunter talked without interruption for fifteen minutes. When he was finished he said, "Well?"

She said, "Come right over."

Hunter tried the door. It was unlocked.

"Anybody home?" he said, stepping aside.

"In the bedroom," Dahlia's voice said.

Hunter locked and bolted the door behind him. On the way to the bedroom he stopped off at the refrigerator for a can of V-8 juice and a beer. He alternated sips from both as he continued down the hall to the bedroom.

"Hi," he said.

Dahlia was in bed. The sheet was pulled up over her breasts and tucked under her arms. She was wearing glasses and reading Thomas Pynchon's *Gravity's Rainbow*.

"What kept you?" she asked.

"This and that." He put the two cans down on the nightstand and unzipped his jacket. He removed the jacket, then the shoulder holster and automatic. He pulled off his sweat shirt and began unbuckling his belt.

"Pretty sure of yourself, huh?" she asked.

"You invited me, didn't you?"

"You didn't give me much choice. You threatened me."

"Threatened you? I asked you; you said okay."

"The threats were implied. What other choice did I have?" Her voice was suddenly loud, but not angry.

"Okay, Hunter, don't move!" A chubby man in a wrinkled gabardine suit was standing in the doorway of the bathroom. A uniformed cop came out of the closet, pointing a shotgun.

Two well-groomed men in suits crowded into the bedroom doorway. "FBI," they chorused.

"I'll handle this," the chubby guy told them. He looked at Hunter. "I'm Lt. Green, cowboy. And this is an ambush."

Hunter stared at Dahlia. "Some bait."

"Don't be too hard on McGuire," Lt. Green said. "She had no choice. We were pretty sure she knew you. It was either cooperate with us or go to jail as an accessory."

Dahlia flipped the covers off. She was wearing jeans but was naked above the waist. She reached for a T-shirt next to the bed and pulled it on. "I don't need you to explain for me, Lieutenant. I made a deal, Hunter. You in exchange for the exclusive story of the capture." She picked up her camera from the dresser and snapped Hunter's picture as they clamped the handcuffs on him.

Hunter jerked away from Lt. Green, catching the fat cop by surprise. With amazing agility for someone with his hands cuffed behind his back, Hunter kicked the cop with the shotgun in the chest. They all heard the snap of cracking ribs.

The FBI agents, Leeds and Harmon, leaped toward Hunter, but he dodged them easily. A leg sweep dumped Lt. Green on his butt onto the floor. Hunter raced for the bedroom door, but when he passed through it, he saw four armed cops pointing service revolvers at him. The loud clack of four hammers being cocked stopped him. Hunter turned just as Dahlia snapped another picture.

"Smile, Hunter," she said. "I'm going to make you famous."

21

Rostov lay on the motel bed and tossed empty peanut shells at the TV screen. Especially at the prissy anchorman who reminded him of a KGB agent who'd once slept with Rostov's wife. Rostov had killed them both with a hockey stick he'd taken from the KGB agent's car. The hockey stick belonged to the agent's fifteen-year-old son. Rostov had been reprimanded, but because he was more valuable than the man he'd killed, nothing was ever done. This anchorman had the same easy smile and sad eyes. Women liked sad eyes, Rostov decided.

". . . as violence continues to sweep the nation," the anchorman said, his eyes shifting slightly as he read the teleprompter. "Every major city in the country has been hit by these savage terrorist attacks. The Soviet Union today denounced such attrocities, but blamed the United States for the inevitable unrest that results from oppressive policies. The President and Congress are considering declaring some form of national martial law. Of course, martial law is already in force in twenty-four states, with more expected by tomorrow.''

Rostov squeezed another peanut shell between thumb and finger until the shell cracked. He dumped the two nuts into his mouth and threw the empty shell at the TV screen. It bounced off the man's forehead.

Footage of some of Rostov's work was being shown: damaged schools, churches, government buildings. Fires. An overturned schoolbus stuffed with dead children. Rostov watched with glee. Surely his superiors were watching, too, rubbing their hands in anticipation of the final fall. Images of destruction were all over the screen: race riots, food riots, religious riots. It was all so easy.

The cost had been great: Tomas, Kurt, Koyo, and now Nikko. Rostov rubbed his wrist, touched the white scar tissue with his finger. But Hunter still lived. And this mission would not be complete until Hunter was dead at Rostov's feet.

''Another strange twist in a week where nothing has been normal,'' the anchorman continued, a sickly smile on his face. ''Miami police working with the FBI finally caught the vigilante who'd been dealing some heavy blows to the terrorists. His name is Matt Hunter. Already Matt Hunter fan clubs have sprung up across the nation. Here's correspondent Lynn Cummings with the story.''

Rostov sat up attentively. The screen filled with pictures of Hunter, handcuffed and in leg irons, being escorted by six uniformed policemen from a squad car to the police station. Crowds of cheering people lined the streets.

The woman reporter brushed a strand of blond hair from her face as she spoke into the microphone: ''. . . As you can see, the alleged vigilante has some strong supporters here. Nevertheless, authorities have transferred him to this

Atlanta hotel, which has been converted into the temporary headquarters of the Southeast Military Assistance Command. Here he will be interrogated by state, federal, military, and civilian agencies before being sent to Washington for—''

Rostov leaped off the bed, scattering peanut shells over the carpet. "No! Once he reaches Washington, I will not be able to get to him." The Russian grabbed his shoulder holster from the closet and strapped it on. Now that he knew where Hunter was, he could finally put an end to it. His face burned in anticipation.

Unarmed, hands cuffed, legs clamped in iron, Hunter was just where Rostov wanted him. It would be like going into a fine restaurant and selecting your own live lobster. Only this way you got to kill it too.

22

Fritz Hanneman kicked the tire of the big armored car. He always kicked the tire of No. 97. Just like when he walked a beat in downtown Atlanta, strolling up Decatur, down West Peachtree past the post office. He'd always given the hydrant on St. Peter a kick for luck. Now, after twenty-eight years on the force, he was a security guard for the Atlanta Armored Car Company, kicking the shit out of fat, hard tires in a garage filled with forty-two armored cars.

No. 97 was his favorite. It was the oldest one of the bunch. Like him. Any day now he expected some of the drivers to start calling him Pops or something. He swore that the first punk who called him Pops was getting the barrel of his .38 across the ear.

Fritz Hanneman had checked the garage and was on his way back to the main office for some coffee and Hostess donuts, both of which his doctor had told him to give up, when the explosion tore the doors off the front of the garage. Fritz drew his .38 and aimed it at the thick billows of smoke rolling inward toward him. He could barely make out the six black-clad figures rushing through the dense cloud. He fired at them anyway.

One shot. That's all he managed to get off. It missed all six men, burying itself in the field outside the garage. He was squeezing off his second shot when Rostov stepped out of the smoke and fired a burst with his Ingram, smashing the transistor radio in Fritz's breast pocket before continuing through the chest and heart.

"Let's go!" Rostov hollered to his men. Seventy-three armed terrorists jogged into the large garage, piling into the backs of various armored cars. "Hurry! Hurry!" Rostov urged.

Carlos Puma, hand-picked by Castro himself for this mission, shook his head at Rostov. "This is a costly setback, Mikal Rostov. We have had to pull men in from all over. Other missions are being neglected. All for one man whom the authorities already have locked up. He can be no threat to us now."

"That is my decision to make," Rostov said.

"Yes. For now. But if anything goes wrong, you must bear the responsibility."

Rostov smiled. "You talk too much, Carlos." He pivoted and fired a three-round burst into Carlos's stomach. Carlos looked shocked, even as he slumped to the cement floor, dead. "I said to *hurry!*" Rostov yelled to the others. They did.

Once all the trucks were loaded, Rostov waved them out toward their destination. Eight terrorists chosen by Rostov remained behind with him. They climbed into two cars and drove to the nearby private airfield where Rostov's look-alike National Guard Huey helicopter was hidden. The nine men boarded.

Rostov pushed the pilot aside. "I'll do it."

"Yes, sir," the man said, the image of Carlos's crumpled body still in his mind. He scooted over to the co-pilot's seat and snapped the headphones over his ears.

Within minutes they were airborne. From the air, Rostov could see the line of seven armored cars speeding through Atlanta.

"He is mine," he whispered, rubbing his wrist. "Finally."

"There, sir." The co-pilot pointed. "There is the hotel."

Rostov nodded. "Let's wait a minute. See what happens."

The helicopter hovered above the hotel. All nine men watched the seven armored cars approach the hotel from different streets. A line of National Guardsmen crouching behind sandbags ringed the hotel. Several sharpshooters were stationed on the roof.

The stolen armored cars blasted through the sandbags. Terrorists opened fire from the gunslots. The guardsmen returned fire, but to no avail. A few were mowed down right away. Others ran.

"Look at them run." Rostov laughed. "Soldiers, hah!"

The armored cars opened up and the terrorists poured out in a swarm, yelling, almost chanting. The sharpshooters on the roof picked off a few, but then Rostov dipped the copter so a couple of his men could blast them away with a few grenades.

When Rostov saw his men charging into the hotel, he smiled. "Take over," he told the co-pilot. "Land us there, on the hotel roof."

While the co-pilot followed orders, Rostov lifted up his M-16 rifle with the M-203 grenade launcher attached under the barrel. He grabbed a handful of grenades and stuffed them into his jacket pockets. He liked the feel of them on his body, the feel of such lethal power draped about him like so much jewelry. Only better than diamonds; 40mm grenades with a muzzle velocity of seventy-one meters, smokeless and flashless, 35g of explosive formed of rectangular-wrapped steel wire, notched for fragmentation. He patted his gun like a pet as the helicopter bounced onto the roof.

"Go! Go!" Rostov yelled as he jumped out. The eight trained terrorists followed.

Rostov slapped a small ball of plastique onto the roof door, blew it, and led the charge down the stairwell. The sound of their boots stomping on metal boomed like church bells. They kicked open the door to the top floor. All the room doors were open. They ran down the hall, checking each room.

Empty.

Rostov led them down to the next floor. That too was empty.

And downward they checked each floor, each empty, until they met their own men who'd been working their way upwards from the bottom. Rostov stood in the middle of the hallway surrounded by seventy-two puzzled men. His face felt hot and prickly as anger washed over him like molten lava.

"Rostov!" one of his men yelled from inside a room. "Come quickly!"

Rostov ran into the room, followed by half a dozen men. One of the terrorists was pointing frantically out the window.

Rostov looked. Two tanks were parked outside. They were adjusting their gun turrets, aiming at the hotel. Around the tanks stood at least a hundred guardsmen. Another hundred were running around the corner of the hotel, probably to the back exits.

"That son of a bitch!" Rostov raged. "It's a trap!"

At those words the terrorists broke into a run. They raced for the exits, clambering down the stairs. Rostov watched as they spilled out of the hotel, only to be cut down by the waiting guardsmen.

"They won't last long," he said to the eight who had remained behind, the eight from the helicopter. "But they will give us enough time to get to the roof and escape in our helicopter. Hurry!"

The men nodded and followed Rostov down the hall and up the stairs. They'd climbed two flights when Hunter's voice boomed at them, echoing down the stairwell: "What time is it, Rostov?"

Rostov flinched, his throat contracting with hatred. "He's here! He's here! You four take this floor," he directed his men. "You other four follow me to the next floor. Find Hunter!"

The first four men kicked open the door to the fourteenth floor, immediately sending a spray of bullets chasing down the hallway.

Rostov and his four men did the same thing to the fifteenth floor. There was no return fire. They had checked three rooms and a luxury suite when they heard the loud exchange of gunfire on the floor below.

"He's downstairs!" Rostov said, running back down the hall. His men followed, exchanging nervous glances.

Rostov leaped down one flight of stairs and burst through the door. His men were only a few feet behind him.

There in the middle of the hallway, the four dead terrorists were arranged to form a large H.

"What time is it, Rostov?" Hunter's voice taunted from the opposite end of the hall.

Rostov made some animal cry as he charged down the corridor, his gun poised and ready. The hallway curved around to another bunch of rooms, the ones that were a little cheaper because they offered no view. Rostov flattened himself against the wall. His men did the same.

"You two will take the rooms on the right. You two will take the rooms on the left with me."

One of the men spoke up. "Sir, what about the helicopter on the roof?"

"First this. We have him cornered."

The men nodded uncertainly, but followed instructions.

The two Rostov had commanded to search the rooms on the right had swept two rooms before Hunter popped out of a bathroom and riddled them both with 9mm bullets.

Rostov and his henchmen charged into the room moments later, but Hunter was already gone.

"Find him!" Rostov screamed again, his neck bulging with blue veins.

Rostov and one of the terrorists searched the next room while the third man kept watch in the hallway.

The guard stood nervously next to the door, his sweaty finger tensed on the trigger. His mouth was dry and tasted bitter. He thought he heard a noise down the hall and swung around to look, his gun snapping to his shoulder. There was nothing. But when he turned back, a large hand clamped over his mouth and another wrapped around his head. The two hands pushed and pulled in opposite directions until the man heard his neck crackle. Then there was an explosion of light in his brain, like someone throwing a log on a dying fire when the sparks leap into the night air. And then nothing.

Rostov and the remaining terrorist discovered the body a full minute after Hunter had killed him. Rostov's anger was almost rabid now, his body movements jerky and anxious. Outside, the constant buzzing of gunfire continued, though it was dying out as the terrorists' ranks grew thinner.

"Rostov?" Hunter's voice called. "Know the time?"

Rostov opened fire with the M-16, chewing up the wallpaper all the way down the hall. He switched the gun to grenade-launcher mode and fired. The grenade blew a hole in the wall at the end of the hallway.

"Thanks," Hunter's voice said. "I think my watch was running a little fast."

Rostov and the last terrorist crept along the wall. The doors to the rooms had all been closed in this section, though they'd been open when Rostov came through the first time. Rostov signaled with his head for the terrorist to break down one of the room doors. The man nodded and swallowed hard. He walked over to the door, took a deep breath, then lifted his leg to kick it open.

Suddenly half a dozen bullets pierced the door and shoved his body backwards into the wall next to Rostov. Rostov quickly dropped to the floor as another dozen bullets chopped through the wall where he'd just been standing.

Then silence.

Rostov loaded another grenade and fired it at the door. The door disintegrated in a puff of fire and splinters. Rostov stuck another grenade in the launcher and ran into the room spraying everywhere with his M-16.

"Just you and me now," Hunter's voice said from the hallway.

The shooting outside had stopped. Rostov looked out

the window of the room and saw the last of his army being marched away, hands on their heads.

Rostov ran out of the room, leaping over the destroyed door. Only midway through his leap, a gunstock swung around and clipped him in the jaw. He felt his jawbone crack and shift painfully to the right as he dropped to the floor.

Hunter stood over him, his H&K SMG pointed at the back of Rostov's head. "Miss me?"

Rostov appeared groggy as he pushed himself slowly to his knees. But then suddenly he kicked out with his right foot and caught Hunter in the kneecap. Hunter toppled backwards, slamming into the wall, the SMG flying out of his hands.

Rostov dove for it. Hunter snagged his ankle and dragged him back across the carpet. Rostov's fingernails clawed at the gun, but no use. Hunter was too strong. Instead, Rostov twisted around and clamped both hands around Hunter's throat, digging his thumbs into his enemy's windpipe.

Hunter sucked for air, but none would come. He pried at Rostov's fingers, but the man's strength was no longer human. Hunter looked into the terrorist's face, saw the hatred in his contorted features.

Hunter felt the dizziness coming over him, the edge of blackness seeping in around the corners of his eyes like a slowly drawn curtain. He had to do something. Now.

He brought his hands out and clapped them hard over Rostov's ears, bursting the terrorist's eardrums. Rostov fell back and Hunter slammed an elbow into his temple, knocking him flat on his back.

Hunter scrambled for the closest gun, Rostov's, while the Russian managed to roll back through the doorway and pull a knife from his boot. Hunter stood in the doorway. Rostov was framed by the window, the knife in his hand like some magic wand.

Hunter shook his head. "Now it's time to die."

Rostov flipped his knife so that he held it by the blade in a throwing position. He cocked his arm back.

Hunter fired the grenade. It thudded into Rostov's chest, exploding bone and tissue in a whoosh of flame. Blood sizzled as opened veins doused the flames. The impact lifted Rostov off his feet and rammed him backwards through the window. The sudden rush of oxygen fed the flames as he fell to the Atlanta streets like a small meteor.

23

"How's the gumbo?" Hunter asked.

Dahlia fanned her mouth as she swallowed. "Spicy."

"Yeah. Perfect."

Mama D waddled over to Hunter's table and slapped him on the back. Her black face was covered with sweat from cooking. "You some hero, boy." She laughed. "Make this place famous."

"I'd never do that to you, Mama D," Hunter said. "I know how much you hate money."

Mama D laughed harder, bending over at her thick waist. "Boy, you don't know Mama D any better than you knew your physics back in school." In perfect Mandarin Chinese she added, "This babe is a live one. Spicier than the gumbo."

"Don't get nosy, Mama D," Hunter said in English.

Mama D laughed again, still talking as she walked away: "I don't know nothin' 'cept cooking. Uh-huh."

Dahlia leaned over and tapped Hunter's hand. "What'd she just say? What was that, Japanese?"

"Chinese. She said you were charming."

"Perceptive, isn't she?" Dahlia smiled. "Where'd she learn to speak Chinese? She work in a Chinese restaurant?"

"No, but she ate in plenty. She was one of the first Americans invited to mainland China after Nixon's visit."

Dahlia looked into her bowl. "Her gumbo's good, but not that good."

Hunter laughed. They ate in silence for a while.

"One thing's been bothering me," Dahlia finally said. "Did you have to break that cop's ribs? I mean, couldn't you just have surrendered like we'd planned?"

"I had to make it look real. The FBI and Lt. Green were in on it, thanks to your persuasive powers, but we couldn't risk anyone else guessing. We had to convince Rostov."

"Well, the cop's fine, in case you're interested. And Officer Mandy's his name, in case you're interested."

"Yeah? Thanks."

They ate in silence again.

"You puzzle me, Hunter. I'm not totally sure whether you're a bad guy or a good guy."

A voice over her shoulder said, "Welcome to the club."

Dahlia turned around. Adams stood there, his beige suit immaculate.

"Dahlia McGuire, meet Adams."

"We've met," she said. "You have a first name, Adams?"

"Not that I like."

"Okay, Adams it is."

He dragged a rickety wooden chair from another table and joined them.

"How goes the war?" Hunter asked.

"All over but the international name-calling. Most of the terrorists have been rounded up. The rest are trying to sneak out of the country any way they can. I'm a big hero for breaking the back of their campaign."

Hunter snorted. "You deserve the credit."

Adams smiled. "That's what I told them too."

"Like little kids," Dahlia said, shaking her head.

"By the way, Matt. Officer Mandy says to thank you for dropping by. He appreciated the visit and the explanation to his family. His kids were thrilled."

Dahlia kicked Hunter under the table. "Why didn't you tell me?"

Hunter ignored her. "What's being done to prevent this from happening again?"

"Officially? Federal investigation groups have been formed, studies are being made, remedies will be proposed."

"That should take five years. What about unofficially?"

"We're setting up a little squad of specially trained anti-terrorists. Go anywhere, anytime."

"A hit squad?" Dahlia asked, reaching for her notebook.

"Of course, Ms. McGuire, if you print any of this it will be denied by everyone."

She looked at Hunter for support. He kept eating.

"So that's how it is," she said, disgusted. "Spooks stick together."

Adams turned back to Hunter. "Anyway, they're looking for someone to head this little elite squad, train them into the best and the brightest. Naturally they came to me first, but I turned the job down."

Hunter plopped his spoon in his bowl and shook his head. "Don't ask."

"I've got to, buddy. They want you to run the whole operation. With me as your faithful companion."

"No way." Hunter stood up, threw down a twenty-dollar bill. "Have a bowl of gumbo on me." He held out his hand to Dahlia. She took it and stood up. They started walking toward the door.

"You'll be back," Adams said. "You like the action."

Hunter didn't answer. He guided Dahlia outside into the warm Miami night. Christmas lights flashed from the street lamps.

"Are you going back?" Dahlia asked.

Hunter put his arm around her and kissed her lightly on the lips. "Not tonight."

LEWIS PERDUE

THE DELPHI BETRAYAL
From the depths of a small, windowless room in the bowels of
the White House, an awesome conspiracy to create economic
chaos and bring the entire world to its knees is unleashed.
☐ 42393-4 THE DELPHI BETRAYAL $3.50

QUEENS GATE RECKONING
A wounded CIA operative and a defecting Soviet ballerina hurtle
toward the hour of reckoning as they race the clock to circum-
vent twin assassinations that will explode the balance of power.
☐ 41436-6 QUEENS GATE RECKONING $3.50

THE DA VINCI LEGACY
A famous Da Vinci whiz, Curtis Davis, tries to uncover the truth
behind the missing pages of an ancient manuscript which could
tip the balance of world power toward whoever possesses it.
☐ 41762-4 THE DA VINCI LEGACY $3.50

the EXECUTIONER by Don Pendleton

Relax...and enjoy more of America's #1 bestselling action/adventure series!
Over 25 million copies in print!

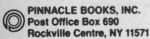

CELEBRATING 14 YEARS IN PRINT
AND OVER 24 MILLION COPIES SOLD!

Buy them at your local bookstore or use this handy coupon

Clip and mail this page with your order